Jake watched her with serious eyes

It was as if in that brief moment he could see right through her to the places that mattered and held the greatest truths. Rachel's heart skipped a beat, and her soul brightened the way sunshine did after passing clouds.

The earth seemed to still and she saw the man he was, beyond the warrior and her brother's friend and Sally's uncle. Jake was no longer a stranger. She couldn't say exactly why; it was only something she could feel. Like faith. Or like hope.

She could sense the heart of the man, his integrity and character and strength. And his goodness.

He folded his strong arms over his broad chest. "Come join me."

That sounded like the best idea ever.

JILLIAN HART

makes her home in Washington State, where she has lived most of her life. When Jillian is not hard at work on her next story, she loves to read, go to lunch with her friends and spend quiet evenings with her family.

JILLIAN HART

Blessed Vows

Steeple Hill®

Published by Steeple Hill Books™

STEEPLE HILL BOOKS

Steeple
Hill®

RECYCLED PAPER · RECYCLED PAPER

ISBN 0-373-87337-9

BLESSED VOWS

Copyright © 2005 by Jill Strickler

This edition published by arrangement with Steeple Hill Books.

® and TM are trademarks of Steeple Hill Books, used under license. Trademarks indicated with ® are registered in the United States Patent and Trademark Office, the Canadian Trade Marks Office and in other countries.

www.SteepleHill.com

Printed in U.S.A.

My purpose is that they may be encouraged
in heart and united in love.
—*Colossians* 2:2

Chapter One

How did she get talked into this? Rachel McKaslin asked herself as she peered into the basement's deep-box freezer. The answer was easy—because she had a teeny-weeny problem saying no. Especially when it came to saying no to any member of her family.

Which was why she was hanging nearly upside down in the freezer and freezing. Her fingertips were numb from shoving packages around. There was a roast in here somewhere. She knew it was in here. But could she find it? No. She did manage to find everything else, though: packages of hot dogs, boxes of frozen fish fillets, bags of frozen vegetables and a big sack of ice pops. The Popsicles she'd been looking for the last time she'd been searching through this freezer.

Wasn't that just her luck?

She grabbed a couple of grape Popsicles and heaved

herself over the edge of the freezer. Her feet hit the ground—yes, she loved being short—and she rubbed the small of her back. A home-cooked meal, that's what her brother Ben had requested for his military buddy, who'd apparently been eating more MREs than real food for the last few years.

Okay. Frozen fish fingers probably didn't exactly qualify as the main course of an old-fashioned home-cooked meal.

It would have helped if Ben had called while she'd still been at work at the diner. She could have made up something right there to bring home. Or she could have stopped by the store and bought a roast like the one she couldn't manage to find now.

Maybe it was time to call in reinforcements. Maybe her sister Paige could send someone over from the diner with a to-go box. And after putting in a twelve-hour day on her feet, she'd be more than glad to give that a try.

It wasn't as if she could cook a roast that wasn't here. Ben would understand. But would his best friend?

She sighed. Well, with her luck, probably not.

She closed the freezer lid, flicked out the overhead light and at the base of the narrow stairs rising up out of the basement, she could hear the *briiing* of the phone.

Great, how long had it been ringing? She imagined Paige calling, worrying about why Rachel hadn't answered after the twenty-seventh ring. Paige was a worrier. Or maybe it was her sister Amy checking in from her latest househunting quest. Or Ben—if it was Ben, then she could explain about the failed roast recovery mission.

She tried to dash up the stairs, but her bunny slippers on the narrow steps slowed her down. By the time she flew up and into the kitchen and wrapped her hand around the receiver, the ringing died. The dial tone droned in her ear. And she didn't have caller ID.

Her cell phone began to chime the opening bars to "Ode to Joy." Excellent! Whoever had called was trying her other phone. Except, where was it? As the electronic music grew louder and louder, she followed the sound into the kitchen and to the round oak table where her duffel bag sat, still zipped. She dug around until she found it.

And it was still ringing. Whew. She flipped it open. "Hello?"

"Ah, is this Rachel McKaslin?" a man's gravelly voice asked, as if uncertain he had the right number.

A man's voice she didn't recognize. *I think I know who this is.* "Yep, that's me." She yanked open the freezer door on the fridge. "Is this Jake, by chance?"

"That would be me. Your brother told you I was comin', but did he warn you about me?" There was a smile to Jake's voice.

Without a doubt a very handsome smile, she thought as she tossed the ice pops into the freezer section of the fridge for later consumption. "Yep, he sure did. The question is, did Ben warn you about *me?*"

His warm, easy chuckle came across the line. "He did. Ben said that you are the generous and lovely soul who agreed to look after us at the last minute *and* on a Friday night. I take that to mean you cancelled a date?"

"Who, me? Date?" She bit her bottom lip to keep in the snicker.

"Well, it *is* a date night, and I understand you're a single attractive lady."

Yeah, right. Not since high school. There were a lot of great men in the world, good and decent men. She firmly believed that, but they never seemed to be interested in her. Maybe it was because she was always so busy, and that didn't leave a lot of time to date. But that didn't explain why no one ever asked her out. Most men were looking for a more worldly woman and, as she looked down at her fuzzy pink bunny slippers, she was anything but worldly.

"I thought I'd sacrifice a date night for Ben's best buddy," she said diplomatically so he wouldn't know he was wrong, wrong, wrong about her. The reason why she was about to be a bridesmaid for the umpteenth time, and not a bride. "It's the least I can do for the man who braved machine-gun fire to help haul my brother to cover a while back."

"He was shot. I couldn't just leave him there for the enemy to trip over."

"My family and I, we're all so grateful to you." Rachel couldn't imagine the kind of courage it took for someone to do their job in the military. "Because of you, our brother's home safe and sound."

"You're giving me a lot of credit. I was just doin' my job. And Ben's a pretty tough guy. I should know, since we serve together. It takes more than a bullet to stop him."

Humble, with a sense of humor. Judging by the deep rumbling baritone of his voice, Rachel figured that Jake had a drop-dead handsome face to match his charm, his smile and his voice. Which meant he was far, far out of her league.

Too bad. She sighed, not really disappointed. She had resigned herself to her unmarried status. She trusted God's plan for her life. Maybe she wouldn't always be single. Maybe He was simply making her wait for the very best man.

The thing was, she was getting extremely good at waiting.

"Rachel, can I ask you something?" There was a slight hesitation in his attractive baritone, as if something was wrong.

He's canceling. That's why he was calling at the last minute—not that she blamed him. From his perspective, he was probably imagining that being with his best buddy's over-thirty-year-old spinster sister wasn't the most fun way to spend an evening. As her slippers scuffled along the kitchen floor, she supposed he was right.

It was just as well because the roast she'd planned

to rotisserie was missing in action. "I know Ben probably felt he needed someone to meet you, since you came all this way and he ran off to spend a romantic evening with his bride-to-be. But eating supper here probably wasn't your first choice. I understand if you'd like to cancel."

"Backing out isn't in my nature. The trouble is, I can't get to your house."

"Oh, you're lost."

"That's not my problem. I found my way here from the airport just fine. But getting to your house is harder than you'd think. I'm parked down the way in your driveway."

"You're here?" No way—she hadn't heard anyone come up. Then again, hadn't she just been in the basement nearly upside down in the freezer?

"How long have you been sitting out there without me knowing it?" Rachel headed straight to the sink and yanked the curtain out of the way. She squinted through the long rays of sunlight. The parking area and the gravel lane leading up to it were empty.

"I'm not exactly at the house yet. Look down the road and you'll see my problem."

A break-down? A flat tire, what? She scanned the length of the newly graveled driveway, past the lawn's reach to the point where the tidy white board fencing paralleled the road.

There he was. At least she figured it was him behind the wheel of a bright red SUV. She could barely make out an impression of a tall, dark-haired, wide-shoul-dered man behind the wheel, but with the glare on the windshield it could have been her imagination filling in the details.

So, why was he just parked in the middle of the road for no reason?

Then she saw the giant ungainly brown creature leap into the middle of the road, between the vehicle and the house. The bull moose lowered his massive four-point antlers, and he meant business. He bellowed an ugly, flat-noted call before he pawed the ground with his impressive front hooves.

Moose attack! Rachel dropped the phone and flew out the back door. She grabbed the first thing she passed by and ran full-out down the path, swinging what turned out to be the old kitchen broom.

"Get! Go on!" she waved the yellow bristles in the direction of the stubborn moose.

The creature didn't even bother to turn around. He kept his hind end to her, as if he already knew there was no way she was a threat.

Well, as if she'd let her brother's best friend and res-cuer be bullied by a stubborn old moose! "You can't bully anyone you want. Get out of the road."

Nothing. The moose had dismissed her entirely. In-stead, his unblinking gaze remained on the shiny red ve-hicle that gleamed in the autumn sun. The animal swung his head as if in a challenge and pawed.

Disaster. All Rachel could see was the animal attacking that brand-new vehicle. That wasn't going to happen on her watch. She swung the broom closer to his hind end. "Hey!"

The moose didn't acknowledge her in any way. What he ought to be doing was bolting in fear of a human being with a weapon. Okay, it was a broom, but he was a wild animal. Weren't they afraid of people? "Go! Shoo!"

Nothing. How was she going to help Jake now?

The driver's-side window rasped down. That deliciously low male voice called out, "Need any help?"

"Oh, no. I can handle it."

"I see. You're doing an excellent job."

Was he mocking her? The moose shook his head menacingly, and bowed low, as if preparing to charge.

Okay, this wasn't going well. It would be a shame for the moose to bash up that new vehicle with his antlers, plus scare the city boy half to death. *Lord, a little help would be appreciated.*

The door of the Jeep whipped open and a lean hulk of a man dropped to the ground as if he'd fast-roped from a Black Hawk helicopter. "Shouldn't your pet be in the pasture or something?"

"Oh, he's not a pet. Are you kidding? Who keeps a moose for a pet? He's a wild animal."

And that's why he's not charging you? Jake didn't have a whole lot of experience with moose, but he did know they were dangerous. "Why don't you back off nice and slow?" He caught up a good-sized rock in his hand.

"You're going to hit him with a rock?" the woman with the broom huffed.

"Only to scare him off. Not hurt him." What kind of man did she take him for?

Jake didn't have time to find out because the moose charged. He was a huge creature. Bigger than the Jeep, the moose gained some serious speed with his awkward-looking legs. He could cause real damage if he hit the vehicle...and he'd probably scare little Sally.

Doing what it took to defend his small niece, Jake lobbed the grenade-sized rock. The hunk of granite bounced off the swoop of the moose's right antler, low enough to give him a slight bonk, but not enough to seriously hurt him. Was it enough to stop the beast?

The great animal shook his head, looking a little cross-eyed. That had to hurt.

For good measure, Jake chose a second rock, peering around the door frame to see if the animal was going to run off, regroup for a second attack or, more possibly, turn around and take his anger out on the woman with the pink furry slippers.

Ben's unmarried sister. Part of him couldn't help thinking, no wonder. But that wasn't fair, because she'd obviously not been expecting him so soon. Had she been lounging after a hard workday, maybe? She wore a big shapeless T-shirt with the faded logo of a local college and baggy shorts.

It was hard to get much of a good impression. Especially with her thick chestnut hair sticking in awkward directions and some of it nearly straight up. She wielded the old broom like a martial arts expert.

One thing he had to say about her was that she was no shrinking violet. She boldly marched toward the angry moose and swatted him on the flank with the bristle end of her broom. "Shoo! Go on! You stop being demanding and greedy. I'll feed you when it's time and not a moment sooner."

This animal *wasn't* a pet? Jake watched as the moose shook his head again, no longer threatening. The poor guy looked contrite before he ambled off in the direction of the lawn, as if he were going to wait there for his feed.

Thank the Lord no one was hurt—including the moose. Jake straightened, dropped the rock and considered his unlikely rescuer. Rachel was not what he expected. Ben talked about his sisters a lot, and it had been clear that he was closest to Rachel.

She looked like her picture. Ben had had family pictures in his dorm during their training years and later in his duplex in the years that followed. All of Ben's sisters were pretty. Rachel's picture had always given him the impression of a demure and introverted young woman, an innocent and a wallflower. Not someone who bossed moose around or had a sparkle to her soul that made him keep looking.

"Uncle Jake?" a small, candy-sweet voice asked from the back seat of the Jeep. "I wanna pet the deer."

"It's a moose, Sally baby," he answered without taking his gaze off of Rachel McKaslin as she held her broom like an M-4. "It's a wild animal. We'd be smart to stay back and give it room."

"Oh. All right." Her sigh was a wistful sound of disappointment.

He'd been hearing that sound a lot over the past few days since he'd come to take charge of Sally. He'd been pulled off active duty in Iraq, and he was still in shock.

One day he'd been rescuing a pair of captured marines and the next day he'd been on a cargo plane to the States with the news his sister had been in an accident, had died and been buried. And he was not only the executor of her estate, but the sole remaining family that his little niece had.

The trouble was, he'd been stateside four days, and it hadn't been time enough to settle his sister's estate, and already his colonel wanted to know when he could get back to active duty.

And Sally…how did he comfort a grieving child? He was a rough-and-tumble Special Forces soldier. As a para-rescue jumper, or PJ, he knew how to jump out of an airplane from twenty-five thousand feet, parachute in and set up a perimeter, execute a mission without a single mishap.

He had Sally, but what was he going to do? It had him stumped.

As if he didn't have enough on his mind, the moose was still glaring angrily at the Jeep from his field. Maybe it was the color that was making him so angry. While the animal had backed away, he hadn't backed down. He still swung his head from side to side and pawed the ground. The Jeep was definitely in danger.

But was Rachel?

"You stay belted in, Sally." He shut the door, leaving her safe and considered Rachel McKaslin, his best buddy's little sister. She was out in the open and unconcerned. Did she know the threat? He stalked the good five yards separating them, keeping a close watch on that moose.

Rachel lowered her broom. "I'm sorry. I should have anticipated this. Bullwinkle does this every evening."

"Bullwinkle?"

"It's just what I call him. I should have fed him and the horse earlier, and you wouldn't have been so rudely welcomed."

"I thought you said he wasn't your pet."

"Not a pet, no, more like a sometimes friendly, sometimes not, wild animal who's decided to take up residence around here and chase the horses away from his grain trough. He's a pushy moose."

"Pushy, huh?" Jake paced closer to protect Rachel, watching as the moose lowered his head and started to charge. Great. On a mission, Jake was prepared for every contingency. He just hadn't thought he'd have to be on alert on a simple trip down a gravel driveway. "Want to give me that broom? It looks like he's coming in for round two."

"I can take care of him."

Jake's hand shot out and he had the broom before she could blink.

"Hey! You took my broom."

"I did."

"But it's my moose. I can handle him."

"I'm trained to serve and protect, so I might as well make myself useful." The handle was solid hardwood. He'd excelled at hand-to-hand combat. "Rachel, stay behind me."

"You're a little bossy, too. It's a moose, not war."

"Everything's war, pretty lady." He timed the moose's gait, waited until the huge ungainly creature was coming head-on and then shot out and rapped him on the nose.

Big nostrils flared, the moose skidded to a stop and shook his head.

"That smarted, didn't it?" Jake kept the broom at the ready. "Do you need another smack?"

The moose's eyes rolled in anger.

Uh-oh. "Maybe that wasn't the best course of action. It works with sharks who get a little too aggressive."

"Smacking them in the nose?"

"Yep. It works every time."

"He's pushy, but mostly harmless. All I need to do is get him some grain. Wait here. With you at my back to cover me with a broom, I feel perfectly safe." She sauntered away, as if without a care in the world.

He was a soldier with fifteen years of experience spent in parts of this world few Americans saw. He'd seen evil, touched evil and battled it. Real evil. And he had the scars to prove it. Even remembering made his heart ache.

He was glad that Rachel McKaslin's biggest problem at the moment was her semi-pet moose. There was peace and goodness in this world. It didn't hurt that he got to see a rare glimpse of it before he headed back to guard this country's freedom.

It didn't hurt to see what he was fighting for.

Chapter Two

Could she see Jake from here? Rachel absently unsnapped the grain barrel's lid and stood on tiptoe. Her attention was elsewhere, straining to see across the aisle, through Nugget's box stall and past the open top of the half door.

Nope. No such luck. She saw plenty of sky and maple trees and the lawn in front of the house. But no Jake.

Pity, since he was such a sight. She had the right to look because he hadn't been wearing a wedding ring. He was pleasing to the eye, pleasing in the way God intended a man to be. But there was more to him, and that was the attractive part—Mr. Jake Hathaway, Special Forces hero, defending and protecting.

He sure had seemed to be in control. He had to be to participate in all kinds of secret missions in the military.

Handling a moose was no challenge for him. He'd tossed that rock as easily as if he'd been skimming stones on a pond and expertly enough so that he'd winged the animal on his antler and hadn't caused any real harm.

And just what did he think of her? *Please, don't let him think I'm a nut bar.* She rolled her eyes as she removed the lid and reached for the scoop. She was still wearing her fuzzy bunny slippers!

She hadn't had a chance to run a brush through her hair or change out of her comfy after-work clothes. So she wasn't exactly looking her best; she was more like looking her worst.

Great way to make a first impression.

This was the reason she didn't have a boyfriend. She kept scaring them off. That was why she made sure, when she prayed for the right man to come along, that he have a sense of humor.

He would definitely need it.

She grabbed a pail from the shelf, dumped in three scoops of sweet-smelling grain and sealed the bin. Nugget was leaning over the side doorway, nickering in hopes of an early supper, poor guy. After leaving him with promises of grain to come, she hurried with the small bucket down the aisle and crawled through the paddock fence that faced the driveway.

Jake was still wielding the broom defensively, but the moose was a little farther off with his head down and snorting. Obviously there had been some action while she'd been in the barn. Before the big creature could charge again, she held the pail high and shook it.

The resulting ring of grain striking the side of the bucket brought the moose's head up. He studied the bright red Jeep gleaming like a big bull's-eye, and then turned to look at the bucket she held. To help him along with his decision to choose the grain over the vehicle, she shook the pail harder and hurried toward him.

"Give that to me and stay back." Jake seemed to take his self-assigned role of defender seriously.

Maybe it was because he thought a woman wearing big long-eared slippers might not be tough. Well, she wasn't afraid of a wild moose. She ignored Jake's advice, she was sure it was well meaning, but really, it wasn't as if she hadn't dealt with this situation before. She marched across the road and upended the bucket on the ground. The grain pellets tumbled and rushed into a molasses-scented pile in a bed of wild grasses, and the moose came running.

With her empty bucket banging against her knee, she hurried back onto the graveled lane as the moose attacked the pile as if he hadn't eaten in five weeks.

"A little theatrical for a moose, but he's mostly harmless," she told Jake, who'd rushed to her side looking pretty angry. "He didn't take a liking to your Jeep, though. I'd move it into the garage if I were you, while he's distracted."

"I can't believe you did that." He stood between her and the moose. "You could have been killed. More people are killed every year in the Iditarod by moose than by all other predators combined, including wolves and mountain lions. You might treat him like a pet, but he's still dangerous and unpredictable."

She grabbed hold of her broom and was surprised at how worked up he was. She could sense how he'd been afraid for her safety, that was why he was all agitated. She didn't know why she could feel his emotions or his intent. Maybe she was reading a lot into his behavior, but it was hard to be upset with a man who only wanted to protect her. Even if it was unnecessary, it was well-intentioned.

And wasn't such goodness what she'd been praying for in a man? Not that he was The One, but still, a girl had to hope. "I'll run ahead and open the garage door for you, and I'll fix you a supper to remember. Is it a deal?"

"That's a pretty tall order, but I'd sure appreciate it." He didn't take his steely gaze from the gobbling moose. "I don't get home-cooked dinners very often."

"Then I'll see you at the house."

His attention remained on his adversary as he backed toward his vehicle. "Are you sure you don't want a ride? You'd be safer."

"I don't think so." How could it be safer to be in close quarters with the handsome, hunky, Special Forces soldier?

She glanced over her shoulder before she stepped into

the garage through the side door. She could barely see the driveway over the top of Mom's Climbing Blaze, the shower of red roses nearly hiding Jake's SUV as he guided it forward at a slow pace, as if expecting the worst.

She couldn't see through the glare on the windshield as the Jeep hugged the lazy curve of driveway along the edge of the lawn, but she imagined Jake was watching the road out of the corner of his eye and keeping a close watch on the moose.

All was well. The wild animal stayed crunching away at his diminishing pile of grain, his jowls working overtime. It looked as if the Jeep was out of danger for the time being, so she hit the button and the garage door groaned upward.

Jake's vehicle was right outside, waiting as the door lifted the last bit. The glare on the windshield had lessened and she could see his silhouette behind the wheel. He was tall. Now that she had a chance to think about it, she remembered looking at the upper span of his chest when she'd stood facing him.

He was really tall, she amended. At least six, six-one.

The vehicle rolled to a stop and she hit the button again. The garage door hid the moose from sight. It didn't hurt a girl to dream, Rachel decided as she backed through the threshold that led through the utility room and into the kitchen, sizing up the man.

He definitely looked like a beef-and-potatoes guy.

Maybe she'd take another pass through the freezer and find that roast she knew was in there—

The vehicle's door opened, but it wasn't Jake's door. It was the one directly behind it. What? That didn't make any sense. Jake was still clearly sitting behind the wheel. She could see him perfectly through the windshield with the dome light backlighting him. He sat soldier-straight and commando-powerful.

There was someone else with him? Her brother hadn't mentioned a second buddy coming in for the wedding that she'd have to feed, too. Not that she minded, but… Her thoughts stopped dead at the sight of a little girl climbing down from the back of the SUV.

Jake had a daughter? She was the cutest little thing, all spindly arms and legs and a cloud of chocolate-brown curls. She had to be about seven or eight and stylish in her matching pink-and-teal shirt and shorts set. Matching sandals with tassels decorated her feet, and a pair of pink barrettes were stuck into her thick, beautiful hair. Costume jewelry dangled from her wrist and her neck, and she held a tattered purple bunny that had seen much better days.

Oh, she was a sucker for kids. Suddenly it made sense that she'd found the Popsicles. It was as if one of God's angels was giving her a clue. Now there was a treat waiting for this adorable little girl. Determined to be friends, Rachel gave a little wave. "Hi there. I'm Rachel."

The little girl stared with big, wide, shy eyes and ducked back behind her open door for safety.

I know just how you feel. Rachel had been shy every day of her life. Her heart squeezed for the little girl, who had to be feeling out of her element.

Then Jake emerged, shrinking the cavernous size of the triple garage with his sheer magnetic presence. He held out one big hand, gentle despite his size. "C'mon, Sally baby. This is Ben's sister I told you about."

"'Kay." She took Jake's hand and let him lead her through the garage. The little girl looked resigned and not happy.

Determined to cheer her up, Rachel offered the child her friendliest smile, but the girl intentionally sent her gaze upward, looking around at the various shelves of tools, lawn stuff, Ben's old hunting gear and every imaginable outdoor activity stored overhead in the rafters—from the canoe to the cross-country skis.

Jake, however, did return her grin. He had a nice grin, one that softened the hard granite of his chiseled face and etched dimples into his lean cheeks. "I don't know if Ben mentioned I had Sally in tow with me. I had planned on picking her up after the wedding, but things didn't work out that way."

Oh, divorce, Rachel guessed. Shared custody. That couldn't be easy for anyone involved. "No problem. Life rarely works out the way you think it will. I was just about to defrost a roast." *If I can find it.* "So that will be enough for all three of us. Sally, may I ask you something?"

The little girl nodded, her pretty emerald eyes wide and somber.

"Do you and your bunny want to help me pick out what kind of potatoes to make?"

Another shy nod.

"Excellent. Are you a mashed-potatoes kind of girl? Or do you like Tater Tots?"

"Tater Tots!" Some of her reserve diminished, and she hugged her bunny tight. "Uncle Jake don't know how to make 'em right."

Uncle Jake? Rachel shot a glance at the unlikely uncle closing his door and nudging the child along in front of him. "It takes talent to know how to get Tater Tots just right. Do you like 'em soft and crumbly or crisp?"

"A little crisp but still kinda all soft in the middle, but not so it's still cold."

"Me, too." Since it was hard not to like a man who took the time to spend with his niece, especially on his limited stateside visit, she'd ask his opinion, too. "Are you a Tater Tot man or a mashed?"

"Strictly French fry, but I can make an exception."

"Maybe I can rustle up a few fries for the man who defended us from the dangerous wild moose. A man needs a reward."

Okay, he could tell when someone was amused at his

expense. "You could have told me the thing was more of a pet than a wild dangerous animal. I did ask."

"He's not a pet. He's just…" She shrugged.

"Got your number." It wasn't too hard to see that Rachel was a genuinely nice person. "Okay, I went a little commando. I had Sally to protect. She's been through enough."

"I'm not blaming you, City Boy. I just wondered if you had fun playing with poor Bullwinkle."

"Not so much."

He liked her. He liked the twinkle of humor in her eye. That she was as friendly as could be without batting her eyes at him like a marriage-minded woman. He did not have a great neon sign pasted to his forehead that blinked, "Not married!" He liked that she was easygoing and that she was pretty up close. Very pretty.

And here he'd been dreading this. He'd originally planned to fly in tomorrow morning, bright and early, and do the wedding and fly home, but Sally had changed things. Here he was in town early, and Ben wasn't here to meet him.

He didn't blame his friend. Instead of a rehearsal dinner, the groom had reservations at one of the nicest restaurants in the area to spend a quiet pre-wedding evening with his bride-to-be, and there was no way Jake wanted him to cancel that. But when Ben had suggested this, Jake had felt obligated to accept this invitation. A home-cooked meal would be good for Sally.

Her hand in his felt so small and held on so tightly. There was a surprising strength in her fingers—or maybe it was need. The way she clung to him was an undeniable reminder of the promises he'd just finished making to her. From the day she'd been born, she'd had a sweet little spot in his heart and now that he was the only one left to look after her, he was only more committed. How he was going to keep those promises to her, he didn't know. Not when his job took him to dangerous corners of the world and kept him there.

Rachel had disappeared through a connecting door on the other side of a laundry room—it was a nice set-up. A closet lined one wall and a washer and dryer covered the wall on his right. Through the window he caught a glimpse of the backyard filled with lush green grass and blooming red roses and big yellow-faced flowers in tidy beds. Trees stood on the far side of the lawn, and that's all he saw before he tugged Sally into the kitchen after their hostess.

"Let me get you something," she said from across a spacious country kitchen.

Nice. He didn't know why he thought so, maybe it was because he'd been on Temporary Duty way too long. Home had become a desert base with a tent over his head and food served on a tray.

Everything smelled so good. The floor of fresh pine and the air like cookies. A chipped coffee mug sat on the granite counter stuffed with red roses from the vines outside. Their old-fashioned fragrance took him back to his grandma's house when he was a kid, where he ran wild during the summers on their San Fernando Valley farm. Maybe that was why he felt at ease with the pretty woman in the kitchen, who looked as if she were in her element as she yanked open the fridge door.

"We've got milk, soda, juice. What's your pleasure?" She looked to Sally first. "I have strawberry soda."

"Strawberry!" Sally gave a little leap, taking his hand with her. "Can I, Uncle Jake?" She beamed up at him with those big green eyes and he was helpless. They both knew it.

"Sure." He'd have to figure out how to say no to her eventually; being a parent was a whole world different than being an uncle.

Sorrow stabbed him, swift and unexpected. He couldn't get used to Jeanette being gone. He dealt with death a lot in the military; he'd lost close friends and team members and soldiers he'd admired. But to lose his sister crossing the street on the way to her office, it wasn't right. It wasn't fair to Sally.

"I've got two cartoon cups to pick from." Rachel held the cupboard door open wide, displaying characters he didn't even recognize.

He hadn't watched cartoons since he was a kid. But Sally lit up and chose one with a big dinosaur on it while Rachel took the other one. She popped one can, filled it, foam and all, to the top of the plastic cup and set it on the round oak table to his right.

It was strange, this big kitchen and eating space, with kids' school pictures framed on the walls—the clothes and hairstyles from decades ago. Through the picture window next to the table he saw half of an old-fashioned metal swing set and slide, in good repair, as if someone had painted it not too long ago. "Ben didn't say. Do you live here alone?"

"Yep. It's way too big for me, but the memories here are good ones. What would you like to drink?"

"Ben said you were a waitress. I can see you're probably an excellent one."

"It's a hard job, tougher than people realize. But it's the family business, and I like it because I get to make all the chocolate milk shakes I want." She waited, hand on the refrigerator door, one slim brow lifted in a silent question. "What'll it take to wet your whistle, sir?"

"If you've got root beer in there, I'll be eternally in your debt."

"I'll hold you to that, soldier." With a wink, she reached inside the well-organized fridge and withdrew two more soda cans.

Before she could snag him one of those breakable glasses neatly organized in the cupboard on the shelf above the cartoon cups, he stole the can out of her hand. "I'm not used to being waited on. Put me to work."

"Work?" She looked him up and down, taking in the strong and capable look of him. "Don't tempt me, or I'll take you up on it."

He perused her big pink slippers and her comfy clothes and the fact that she hadn't had time to do up her hair into anything remotely involving hair spray and gels or whatever it was women put in their hair. That said everything. "Did you have other plans before Ben strong-armed you into doing this tonight?"

"Plans with the couch and an old movie. Nothing that can't wait until tomorrow night. Or the next night." She poured the contents of her can into the plastic mug, and the sweet-smelling pink liquid fizzed. "Wait!"

He had hold of the cup the instant she stopped pouring.

"Hey, what are you doing taking my strawberry soda?"

"What? Do you think I'm stealing it from you?"

"That's what it looks like. I call things like I see 'em."

"And what, that look of outrage is because you didn't know you were letting a strawberry soda bandit into your house?"

"That, and you're setting a very bad example for Sally."

"Is that true, Sal?" He sent a wink to his niece, who'd seated herself at the table and was sipping from the cup with both hands.

Her solemn gaze met his over the wide rim. Strawberry soda stained her mouth as she said the words of betrayal. "Stealing's wrong, Uncle Jake."

"Hey, I'm one of the good guys. Or at least that's what they tell me." And because he knew what it was like to put in a long hard workweek, he wasn't about to give up the glass of soda. "How about I wait on you? You said you had a date with the couch?"

"You've got to be joking."

"I never joke, ma'am. I'm an air force commando. Duty is my name."

"Yeah, yeah, you forget I have a brother who spouts that macho stuff all the time." She waved him off as if she knew better, as if she had his number.

Fine. The trouble was, now that he wasn't worrying about a rampaging moose, he could get a real good look at her. He liked what he saw. She was petite, there was no other word for her. Delicate, for lack of a better word. She had the clearest, creamiest skin he'd ever seen, and the gentlest manner.

A real nice woman. He wasn't about to impose on her like a deadbeat. No, he wasn't that kind of man, although he read her look of skepticism loud and clear. That was okay. He wasn't bothered by it.

"Follow me," he said, trusting that she would.

Chapter Three

She did follow him. Jake monitored the pad of her slippers against the carpet a good two to three paces behind him. "That's it. Keep coming."

"I want my strawberry soda back in the kitchen where it belongs." She didn't have a sharp voice or an angry edge. No, she was all softness and warm humor, as if he were amusing her to the nth degree.

He wasn't used to softness and humor, not in his life of duty and service. So, he thought he'd enjoy the chance to amuse her some more. "Is there a house rule about keeping all food and beverages in the kitchen?"

"There is, as a matter of fact."

"Funny. I didn't see a sign."

"It has to be a sign?"

"Sure. If it's not written down, it's not a law I have to follow."

"Yeah? Then for you I'll make an exception."

He liked the rumbling music of her chuckle. It was an appealing sound, one a man could get used to. Nice.

And so was the house, he thought as he stepped inside the sizeable living room. Spacious. Comfortable. It was the kind of place a guy could get used to putting his feet up on that scuffed coffee table that sat in the middle of a big sink-into-me sectional. The TV was big and new, and in the winter this would sure be a great spot to sit and watch football with a fire in the gray rock fireplace.

He used an old television guide as a coaster and left the drink on the coffee table within easy reach. "Sit there. Put your feet up."

"That would be rude considering I'm supposed to be cooking you dinner."

He held out his hand, palm up and waited for her to take it. "C'mon. I'm the guest, right? So humor me."

"My mother taught me to be wary of men wanting to be humored."

"Sounds like your mama raised you right. And so did mine. It may be hard to believe to look at me, but I've got a few manners." He shifted closer to her with his hand still out, still waiting. "What's it going to be? Are you going to do what I ask? Or am I gonna have to make ya?"

"Men." Rachel sized up the commando in her living room, with his dazzling grin and his hand held out, palm up, waiting for her to place her fingers there. "Suddenly I remember why it is that I'm single."

"Those bunny slippers?"

He clearly thought he was a comedian, but he wasn't nearly as funny as he thought. "No, judging by my slippers you might be misled to think men have avoided me on purpose."

"I don't think that, believe me."

"But it's been my choice. Most men are bossy."

"We're made that way."

"Sadly." He didn't seem the least bit sorry about it. He was incorrigible, and she liked that in a man, too. He had nice eyes—kind ones—and she was a sucker for a good-hearted man. How was she going to ever say no to this one?

Willpower, she directed herself. "I'm supposed to be the hostess. You've flown all this way to be Ben's best man. The least I can do is talk you into sitting down and putting up your feet."

"Good luck. But let me warn you, I'm stubborn."

"I'm stubborn, too." There was no way she was going to give in to the temptation to place her fingertips on his big rough palm.

Oh yes, she wanted to. His palm was wide and relaxed, and calluses roughened the skin at the base of his fingers. He worked hard. She liked that in a man too.

His hands had scars—not big ones, just nicks that had long healed over, and those calluses. She imagined him fast-roping from a helicopter or carrying wounded on a litter. Essentially male, wholly masculine, everything a man ought to be.

And suddenly she felt it in the pit of her stomach. A little tingle of anxiety. Her shyness seemed to rear up and leave her speechless. It was one thing to have her brother's military buddy drop by. It was another to be alone with a smart, brave and warm-hearted soldier.

If only she could untie the knot her tongue had gotten itself into and say something wonderful to make him laugh some more. To show off the dimples in his hard, carved cheeks.

"I'm waiting." He arched one brow, but he wasn't intimidating in the least. He should be—he was a big man, and the slightest movement made muscles ripple beneath his sun-bronzed skin.

But he was a gentle giant down deep, Rachel was sure of it. "How about you and Sally sit down with me? We'll find something on the tube that all three of us can enjoy and after a while, I'll sneak into the kitchen and start supper."

"There'll be no sneaking on my watch. I've got a sharp eye." His hand hovered in a silent question.

And she answered just as quietly by placing her fingers in the center of his palm. *Wow.* It was all she could think the instant they touched. An energy jolted through her like a lightning strike—or heaven's touch.

She felt seared all the way to her soul. It was as if

her entire central nervous system short-circuited—she couldn't seem to talk. She could barely manage to be coordinated enough to sit down.

Wow, was all her poor fried brain could think. *Wow. Wow. Wow. Lord, he can't be the one. He* can't *be.* Look how he acted as if nothing had happened. It probably hadn't on his end. She searched his clear dark eyes and the calm steady way he moved away from her with sheer athletic grace as he ambled out of sight.

She'd read about moments like this, that instant punch of something extra that said this man was special. Above the ordinary. Meant to last. Okay, she read inspirational romances one after another. She always had her nose in one, but she'd never believed, never thought once that it could happen to her.

Not that it was a life-changing moment. It was just a snap of something extra, making her more aware of this man's goodness than others she'd come across.

Why? He couldn't be the one. He lived on the other side of the country and he worked in faraway places on other continents. Plus, he was leaving after the wedding.

He's not the one. She was imagining all this, right? She was tired, she hadn't eaten since she'd been able to work in an early sandwich before the lunchtime rush. She was feeling the weight of being a bridesmaid for the umpteenth time. Not that she minded, no way. And especially because this was her brother's wedding.

But she wanted to be a bride. She wanted the real

thing, a sweet storybook wedding with the man she would love for all time. That's why she was feeling this…wishful thinking. Pretty powerful, but wishful thinking all the same.

The pleasant rumble of his voice from the kitchen drew her attention. It was like a tingling warmth in her heart, and she'd never felt that before either. She could hear Sally's answer and then the faint scrape of the wood chair on tile.

That's why I feel so wowed by him. It all made sense now. She loved a man who was good with children. And his niece was a cutie, that was for sure. It was sweet he was spending time with her. And now that she knew why she was so taken with him, it would be easier to keep things in perspective.

"Hey, Rachel." Jake rounded the corner with Sally at his side, her small hand engulfed by his huge one. "Mind if she uses the facilities?"

"First door on the right." Rachel stood, but Jake waved her back and deftly disappeared beyond the edge of the fireplace. In a few seconds, a door closed down the hall.

What she really ought to do was to take another crack at finding that roast. The soda would keep—it was fizzing and bubbling merrily in the cartoon cup.

As for her aching feet, she could get a few more hours out of them, she thought as she cut through the dining room and dashed down the basement steps. Her guests would be busy for a few moments, and if she could just find that roast—

"Running away from me?" Jake's baritone was filled with friendly, warm amusement.

Good thing she wasn't affected. "Not running any farther than the freezer. Why don't you help yourself to the remote? I don't mean to be a bad hostess, I'm just digging stuff out for supper."

"Suppose I help you with that?" His steps sounded behind her on the stairs.

"Oh, I can get things just fine." Actually, what she needed was someone who was tall enough to reach all the way to the bottom of the freezer. Was she going to admit that to him? No. "I'll be right up, okay?"

No answer was forthcoming, although the approaching rasp of sneakers on the cement floor trailed her to the freezer room. Rachel yanked on the light.

And there he was, he'd caught up to her, and let out a breath of awe. "Wow. Did you do all this canning?"

"My sisters lent a hand." She supposed the floor-to-ceiling shelving and all the jars sitting on them did look impressive. "We like to can."

"I'll say."

"It's something our mom used to do. She'd get all of us to help her, even Amy when she was just a preschooler. We'd all peel and cook and fill jars." She reached to open the freezer lid, but his hand was already there, lifting the lid and exposing the icy contents to the glare of the light.

That's how she felt, illuminated in the deep reaches of her self. How could talking about the preserving jars on the shelf do that? Simple, she realized. "It was everything good in our childhoods. Maybe that sounds corny, but the memories are good ones. The kind that really matter."

"That make you who you are?"

His comment surprised her, this tough commando who had lobbed a rock like a grenade in the driveway as if at war. He was understanding, and she decided she liked him even more. "When my sisters and I do our yearly frenzy of making jams and canning, it always brings us back, makes us part again of that time in our childhoods when Mom was alive and her warm laughter seemed to bounce around the kitchen like sunbeams."

Sometimes it hurt to remember, but it hurt even more to forget. And so she remembered. "When Dad would come home with packed meals from the diner because he knew Mom would have been so caught up she'd have forgotten the time. The whole house would smell like the strawberry jelly simmering on the stove, or the bushels of fresh peaches we'd have spent all day sitting around the table slicing."

"Ben said you lost your folks when you were young."

"It was like the sun going out one day." And that was the part of remembering that hurt most, like a spear through the heart. "But Paige was just sixteen then and she took care of us."

"You were alone?"

"We didn't want to be split up, and no one could take on the four of us." Well, the spear remained lodged in her heart and the past was just going to keep hurting if she kept talking about it. She turned her attention—and the conversation—to the freezer. "You wouldn't want to reach down with those long arms of yours and dig around for a roast, would you?"

"A roast. Why, ma'am, I'd do nearly anything for a good roast. We don't get those much in the deserts where I've been spending my time." He leaned down as if to thrust his arm deep into the frosty mists, but stopped in mid-plunge. "I can't believe this. You have my absolute favorite fish sticks. I mean, these are the best."

"I love those, too. They're the best with the tartar we make at the diner. I've got a jar—"

"Forget the roast. Let's whip up a cookie sheet of these, bake up some Tater Tots and I'll be happy as a— Oh boy, you've got real apple pie in here."

"Homemade. If you want—"

"Yeah. Yeah, I do." He loaded up with the pie and the fish sticks before closing the lid. "You really don't mind?"

"Are you kidding? I've been on my feet all day. Tell you what, how long are you staying in town tomorrow?"

"Uh… Don't know. We're on a standby flight back

to LA. I've got the last of the estate stuff to settle, it's a long process." The look on his face, one of grief, one of bewilderment kept her from turning off the light.

Estate stuff? Rachel's stomach twisted. Before she could ask, Jake reached up and snapped off the light, leaving them in shadows. "Sally's mom died—my sister. Hit by a bus on the way to work one morning."

No. That poor little girl. Rachel's heart wrung in sympathy. She knew just what that felt like for a child to lose a mother. "And her father?"

"Nonexistent. Ran off long ago and never wanted to be responsible. No one can even find him now. That's why I have her." He took off abruptly, speaking over his shoulder, sounding normal but his movements looked jerky and tense in the half-light drifting down the staircase. "That's why she's with me. If I hadn't taken her when I arrived home, then she would have had to stay in foster care while I came here. And she asked me not to leave her. So I didn't."

"I'm glad you brought her." Well, that was about the saddest thing she'd heard in a long time. "How long was she alone while you were in the desert?"

"Nearly seven weeks. That's a long time."

"Too long." Rachel's quiet agreement said everything.

I wish I could have gotten to her sooner. There was no getting around that fact. Or the logistical problems of hunting him down in the middle of a covert deployment and getting him back to the States again.

Jake felt the weight of impossible guilt, dragging him downward. He'd done all he could, but it didn't change the fact that Sally had been left alone to grieve in a stranger's home, under a stranger's care, and she wasn't the same little girl he remembered. It was as if something essentially her had died too, of sorrow. How was he going to fix it for her? He didn't have a single answer.

Maybe the Lord would give him one, since he was all out of ideas. All out of everything.

"I'll do what I can to make sure she has some fun," Rachel said.

So much understanding lit her voice, and it struck Jake like a bullet to the heart. He hadn't registered his worries about bringing Sally—about everything. He didn't want to go there. He would handle it, things would work out. He was Special Forces trained to assess, adapt and overcome. He'd succeeded at every training exercise, every task and every mission. But a child was not a mission.

He headed up the stairs, box in hand, not sure if he could look Rachel in the eye. "I figured that since Ben had a nephew about Sally's age, she might not be too out of place."

"Oh, of course not. I happen to be in charge of the kids' activities. You know, receptions are so boring for the little people. All that sitting still and vows and kisses and then the manners at the sit-down meal. So we're going to have our own party outside. I'll take good care of Sally for you. I'm sure you and Ben will want to hang out for a while at the reception."

Jake nearly missed the last step up. "I hadn't thought about pawning her off on anyone. That wasn't what I meant—"

"I know. But I was simply informing you of our plans. If you want her to be with the other kids, we're going to have a lot of fun." Rachel shut the door and followed him to the counter where he'd dropped off the fish box. "We'll have games and races and our own cake. We're having hot dogs and burgers. It's going to be such a blast, I can't wait."

Ben was right. His sister Rachel was the nicest person ever. And she didn't seem to know it, didn't seem aware that she was as incredibly beautiful on the outside as she was on the inside. Her loveliness shone outward like sunlight through clouds, and it dazzled.

He had to turn away, blinking hard, affected and he didn't know why. He was used to keeping his feelings under lock and key. Why his emotions were staging a breakout, he didn't know, but he didn't like it. Not one bit.

Rachel clicked on the oven and there was a clatter as she dug a cookie sheet out of the bottom cabinets. Her "Oops!" was good-natured as she put away the other racks and cookie sheets that had tumbled out with the first one.

She had a patience about her, an inner harmony that he admired. It didn't take a rocket scientist to see that she was probably great with kids. "I'm sure Sally would like to hang out with you tomorrow. Thanks."

"Not a problem." She rose, a petite willow of a woman who moved like poetry, like grace, like all that was good in the world.

It was nice, it was normal. He wasn't used to nice and normal, he'd been away from a normal life for so long, he didn't feel as if he quite fit anymore. It was heartening to see, it gave a man pause, to watch a woman in a kitchen preparing supper and to know all was safe here, all was right in this tiny piece of the world.

Maybe he could lay down his responsibilities, the constant on-guard duty he carried, and rest for a short while. He hadn't realized how tired he was, but it washed over him like a warm rain.

"Jake, I'll whip you up some homemade fries," she said as she hauled real potatoes out of the pantry. "It'll only take a second. Sally is welcome to have her soda in the living room. Why don't I take that in to her before I start getting busy in here?"

His throat closed entirely. Unable to know what emotions were whirling around free inside him, and just as unable to speak, he held up his hand, stopping her with what he hoped wasn't too harsh a gesture and grabbed Sally's cup and his soda can.

He walked out of the kitchen and didn't look back, but he swore he left a part of himself standing there, awed by the woman and her kindness.

Chapter Four

It always made Rachel happy to be in the kitchen. With the hum of the TV drifting in through the dining room, she popped the tray of fish sticks and Tater Tots into the oven and plunked the small hill of hand-cut potatoes into the deep-fryer. Cooking was comforting, maybe because she associated it with her mom and dad.

Few things in a day made her happier than having someone to cook for, even temporarily. The fatigue that had built on her in layers throughout the day began to fade. As she set the timer, a new burst of energy lifted her up. The fryer's oil sizzled and snapped and the sound was a friendly accompaniment while she dug through the shelving inside the refrigerator's door and picked out the appropriate condiments.

After loading up a tray with napkins and flatware, she set out for the living room. The rise and fall of voices from the television grew louder, drawing her closer. On the couch in front of the colorful screen and washed in the glowing light, the big man and little girl sat side by side, intent on the old family movie.

Wow. It was awesome Sally had an uncle like Jake who would take her in without question. Otherwise, she'd hate to think of what the child might face. She'd been exposed to that fear as a kid. But probably Sally had it worse losing her home and having to move across the country to the house where Jake was stationed. While Sally battled her grief over her mom, at least she had Jake to love and protect her, to keep her safe from this world that often did not think of children.

Rachel set the tray in the center of the coffee table, leaning just right so she wouldn't block their view of the tube.

Jake stirred from his TV watching. "I ought to get off my duff and help you."

"There's nothing left to do."

Heaven save me from this man. It would be nothing at all to simply fall fast and hard in love with him. Well, not real love, that was something that deepened forever between a man and woman, but the initial tumble, *that* wouldn't take too much if she kept seeing more of his good heart.

Nope, she needed to handle things from here by herself. It was a matter of self-preservation. "You stay right there with Sally. She needs your company. I'll be back with supper."

"You eat in here?"

"Why not? It's Friday. It's the tradition in this house."

As she turned her back on the cheerful movie flash-ing across the screen, it was the past and its cherished memories that came with her. This was why she loved living in this house so much. The four of them together as kids, crowded onto the two couches that used to be in this room, pushing and shoving and laughing in good humor so that it was hard to listen to the movie.

Dad would be manning the grill outside if it was summer, and he'd pop his head through the slider door and shout at them to stop hitting one another. As she set up the TV trays, Mom would be laughing, reminding him that he was the one who wanted four kids, remem-ber?

As often as not, one of them would jump off the couches to help her. Soon their favorite meal of cheese-burgers and Tater Tots would be served up on the trays, they'd all be eating and watching the TV. All through the show, Dad would make funny comments meant to make them all howl with laughter.

Yeah, she thought as she whipped the fries from the hot grease, this was the reason she hadn't settled down yet. Because she hadn't settled. How could she want anything less than the family life she'd had growing up? One day, the good Lord willing, she would know that brand of happiness again.

Until then, it was nice to dish up plates with everything just right for her guests. Tater Tots done just right—crispy on the outside and warm and chewy on the inside. Fresh fries still steaming, both heaped on half of the good stoneware she'd gotten for Christmas from her sisters, and plenty of golden crispy fish sticks. Small bowls of coleslaw, made fresh at the diner that morning, added the required vegetables to the meal.

The loaded tray made hardly a clatter as she carried it through the dark dining room and into the living room where the bold animation on the screen flashed enough color to light her way. Careful not to disturb the movie-viewing, she handed off Sally's plate, setting it right in front of her on the coffee table and adding the little bowl of coleslaw. She meant to circle around and slip Jake's plate onto the other side, but he held out his hand. "If that tastes as good as it smells, I'm gonna be the most grateful man in Montana."

"You really must be hungry. To be the most grateful man over a pile of fish sticks." She avoided his fingers as she gave him his plate heaped with steaming-hot food and then slid the bowl of slaw onto the coffee table before he could reach.

"Do you know how long it's been since I've had a home-cooked meal?"

"This isn't home cooked. It's straight from the freezer." It was funny he thought so, though.

"These fries look homemade."

"They are, but, well, the rest used to be frozen. But, hey, as long as you're happy."

"Happy? I've spent the last two years nearly straight in the desert. Eating MREs and mess-tent food, and let me tell you, this is the best. Just the best." He sounded as if she'd set an expensive, four-star meal in front of him.

"I'm glad you think so." That was what mattered. If Ben's best buddy was happy, then she was, too. "If your flight doesn't work out, I'll make you that roast dinner tomorrow."

"Deal. You want to say grace?"

"You're the guest." She unloaded her plate onto the corner of the coffee table and set the tray out of the way. "Please, you go right ahead." She was pretty interested in what he'd say. A tough guy, just like her brother, would probably be to the point. Her brother's favorite prayer, she guessed: "Good food, good God. Amen."

Jake's head bowed and his big hands steepled. Definitely not what she expected, but she liked what she saw—the sincere tilt of his profile as his eyes drifted shut.

"Dear Heavenly Father, " he began in his steady baritone. "Thank you for the blessings we find at the end of this day. That Sally and I are together. We have had a safe journey from California and a peaceful solution to Bullwinkle's attack. And most of all, thank you, Lord, for bringing us a new friend in Rachel, and I'm especially grateful for the fish sticks."

His genuineness sounded somehow richer when mixed with his gentle humor, and as Rachel sat with her head bowed, she sneaked a glance at Jake through her eyelashes. He looked totally at ease and comfortable in prayer, and it was clear he had a solid relationship with the Lord.

If he hadn't been sitting next to her on the couch, all one-hundred-percent flesh-and-blood man, she would have figured him to be a daydream she'd woven of the perfect guy. A courageous warrior who served his country. An honest man of strong faith. Kind to children. Funny and handsome and…

Whoa, there, Rache. He's just visiting. As she managed to get out an "Amen" without sounding too distracted, she opened her eyes all the way, unfolded her hands and tried to remind herself that Jake wasn't looking for romance. He was leaving for good after the wedding and she'd never see him again.

Too bad. It was hard not to feel disappointment or a little bit wistful as Jake helped himself to generous spoonfuls of their secret-family-recipe tartar sauce, dragged four fries through it, and took a bite. He moaned even before he started chewing.

"I should have added the tartar to the list of blessings," he quipped, looking about as handsome as any man could with those dimples carved into his lean, sun-browned cheeks.

Her heart gave a little tumble. Of admiration, she

firmly told herself, and not of interest. She fastened her gaze firmly on the TV screen and did her best not to look at Jake and his dimples.

Impossible. He leaned close so that their shoulders were almost touching. Only a scant hairbreadth of air stood between the curve of her shoulder and the hard line of his arm. "The tartar's even better on the fish sticks. I owe you, Rachel."

"Well, I didn't plan on charging for the meal," she joked.

And brought out the warm rumbling chuckle. "I'm doing the dishes and I don't want a single argument from you. Got that, ma'am?"

"Sorry. You're outranked."

"How can you outrank me? You're not a commanding officer. You're not even in the armed services."

"But I have the power to take away the tartar sauce." How she could banter so easily with this man, she didn't know.

She only knew that her chest and heart felt warm when Jake gave her a smile with those full-wattage dimples and leaned close to her ear, so close, his breath tickled hot against the curve of her ear. "Go ahead and try."

"Okay. I will. You watch out, soldier boy." She dunked a Tater Tot into the pile of tartar on her plate, surprised how she didn't feel shy at all. It was as if she'd been bantering with this man all of her life.

* * *

The brilliance of the September sunset came like peace to the evening. Rachel paused at the sliding door just to take in the awe of magenta streaks painting the sky and bold purple splashes staining the underbellies of the clouds. The colors glowed so brightly in the off-blue sky that the shadows streaking across the back lawn from the tall stand of trees at the property line were amethyst and an incredible rose light graced them.

Why this evening's sunset seemed particularly glorious, she couldn't rightly say. Especially when she'd been so beat after a long rough workweek and those last-minute, nerve-racking wedding preparations. Maybe it was the fish sticks and Tater Tots, which were one of those childhood favorites Mom used to make for them when Dad was working late at the diner. Good memories from her childhood always heartened her.

But having Jake and Sally here in this house had lifted her up, too. Having a child in this house, watching an animated movie and now swinging on the swing set in the big backyard stirred a longing inside her. Cooking for a man and child, even people she would never see again after tomorrow, made her wish for her own husband and child.

Maybe it was that over-thirty thing—the biological clock everyone talked about—but watching Jake give Sally a hard push on the swing, sending the girl soaring up high, made her realize how lonely her life was.

Sure, she had a great family, she had a great job and she loved this life God had given her, but her heart was lonely for a man, someone strong and kind and good like Jake, and a little child to love and care for.

She knew if Jake and Sally hadn't come tonight, the sounds of laughter wouldn't be shimmering like the rosy light in the air. She would have come home, collapsed in front of the TV and eaten leftovers from the diner, then she would have done a few loads of laundry, caught up on the housework and probably started watering the yard. All the while the big house would have been echoing around her with the memories of family happiness in the past and none for the future.

She was beginning to think the Lord had forgotten about her deepest, most precious prayers. Or maybe He meant for her always to be alone. She hadn't minded it so much because she'd been so busy helping her sister Amy take care of her son Westin; having a nephew to dote on had filled her heart and her life enough that she didn't hurt for her own family so much.

And now, Amy had gone and gotten married, which was a great blessing to their family. She'd found a good man who cherished her and Westin, and was always eager to help with anything the family needed. Amy's new husband Heath spent a lot of time with Westin, and while Rachel was utterly thankful for that, she didn't see Westin as much.

Why tonight the loneliness felt so keen, like the crisp

edge of light too brilliant to look at, she didn't know. Only she had tears burning behind her eyes and a pain like a blade slicing her heart, and there was no reason for it. Not when she had so much already in her life.

Jake gave Sally another push and paused to watch his niece shrieking with delight as she swept up toward the sky. "Rachel McKaslin. Have I told you why you're my most favorite person?"

"It wouldn't be because I'm holding grape Popsicles, would it?"

"Pretty much. You just know where to hit a guy."

"Oh, you're wrong there. I never hit. So, are you telling me that there's truth to the old saying? The way to a man's heart is through his stomach?"

"I don't know about the heart, but a grape Popsicle will put you at the top of my list." He stepped back in time with Sally's swing as she zoomed backward between them.

There was something awesome about a big tough man being tender with a child. Rachel waited tongue-tied as he gave Sally a big push.

The little girl squealed with joy. "Are those grape?" she shouted as she swept backward between them.

Rachel managed to nod, and the fact that she couldn't seem to speak didn't matter as Sally dug the heels of her little sandals into the grass to slow the swing.

"Is that for me?"

"Yep. I hope you like grape."

"It's only like my very most favorite!"

Rachel's heart melted at the sight of the little girl, an orphan and grieving the loss of her parent. Finding the Popsicles in the crowded freezer had seemed like a small thing at the time, and yet Rachel could see God working in her life as clearly as the tentative grin on the little girl's sweet face. "Grape is my favorite, too. Here you go. Be careful, because it's already melting."

Sally took the plastic bowl eagerly with one hand and grabbed hold of the wooden stick handles with the other. She'd been such a quiet little girl until now, more of a shadow than a child, and it was good to see the hint of the child Sally must have been before her mother's death.

And because she knew exactly how that felt, she added a silent prayer. *Dear Father, I know that you're watching over her. Please keep watching over her.*

When she opened her eyes, she realized Jake had stepped away from the swing and was sitting on the closest picnic table bench, watching her with serious eyes.

It was as if in that brief moment he could see right through her to the places that mattered and held the greatest truths. Her heart skipped a beat and her soul brightened the way sunshine brightens the day after passing clouds.

In that moment it was as if the earth stilled and time halted and she saw the man he was; she saw beyond the warrior and her brother's friend and Sally's uncle. Jake was no longer a stranger. She couldn't say exactly why; it was only something she could feel. Like faith. Or like hope.

She could sense the heart of the man, his integrity and character and strength. And his goodness.

He folded his strong arms over his broad chest. "Come join me."

That sounded like the best idea ever. Her feet were moving her forward before she made the conscious decision. "Sally seems to be having a good time. I'm glad you brought her."

He took the bowl she offered him. "Being here seems to have done her a world of good. I haven't seen her smile since I came to pick her up. Now I owe you."

"For what?" She eased onto the far end of the bench. "I didn't do anything. Just made supper and apple pie and now I handed her a Popsicle."

"Ben told me you were humble, too. Not just nice and sweet and funny—"

"My brother is biased, plus he spends most of his time far away from here. You know that. Distance makes the heart grow fonder and dulls the memory of a person's faults."

"Sure, okay. I don't buy that." He bit off the end of his Popsicle. "You are funny."

"Me? I haven't said anything funny since you got here. I wish I were funny. You know, like a comedian."

"Well, you are the only woman I know who wears big pink rabbits on her feet."

"What?" She stared at her slippers. She was still wearing them? "I'd forgotten all about them."

"And you're nice. You could have let your pet moose attack me and Sal."

"It was tempting." She slurped the melting goodness off the top of her grape pop. "Like I said, I owed you for saving Ben when he was hurt."

"He seems to be doing better. They say he'll be back on base after his honeymoon."

"He's pretty psyched about being able to return to active duty."

"We're pretty psyched he's coming back. He might get back to work before I do." Jake nodded to where Sally sat twirling in the swing while licking the dripping goodness of the iced treat. There was a whole lot he didn't know how to say. His job wasn't just any job. He was a para-rescueman; he put his life on the line so that others might live. And he couldn't do that living near the base and being home every night to take care of Sally.

And yet if he didn't take her, then there was no one else but social services. He wouldn't do that to her. He couldn't. He loved her too much and he could never break the trust his sister had placed in him for Sally's sake.

Lord, I know this is all in Your plan. So please, show

me the way to help Sally through this. Show me what I'm supposed to do with her and for her.

Jake had no idea how this was going to work out. He had orders to be back at Hurlburt by the end of the month. He fully expected to be deployed immediately. He'd rejoin his squad in the Middle East. Orders were orders, and how he was going to do his duty and be home to take care of Sally was a mystery. Was there a chance he could find someone trustworthy to take care of Sally while he was gone? A good nanny was his only option.

"I imagine having her in your life is going to change things a bit." Understanding shone in Rachel's lovely blue eyes, as if she could see his dilemma.

She was so friendly and kind, it was hard to remember he'd only just met her today. Maybe it was because he knew Ben so well and he'd seen the family pictures—with Rachel in them—that Ben had, as long ago as the tough seven weeks of PJ qualifications at Indoc that made boot camp look like a day at the beach. Whatever it was—probably God's hand in things—he felt as if he'd known Rachel far longer. And that she was someone he could trust. That was something he hadn't had in a real long time.

"I'm lucky I have my own place off base. Ben lives in the same complex."

"Are you on the beach, too?"

"Oh, yeah. Not that I'm ever home to enjoy it. But

at least I've got a roof and four walls and a bedroom to get fixed up for her." He bit into the sugary grape ice and savored the blast of flavor on his tongue. "First I've got to get her settled. Make her feel like she's got a home no matter what."

"That will mean a lot to her."

The gentle evening breeze gusted, catching wisps of Rachel's beautiful hair. The rich chestnut strands were shot with gold from the soft rosy evening's light and caressed the side of her face, emphasizing the creamy complexion of her skin and the delicate cut of her high cheekbones. Hers was a beautiful face, he realized. So lovely that he could not look away.

She seemed unaware of her beauty—both outward and inward—as she bit into her iced pop and watched Sally on the swing. She tilted her head to one side, her hair sweeping against the delicate arch of her neck. The breeze stirred between them, bringing him the scents of grape and a subtle sweet cinnamon scent.

"It's going to be a huge adjustment for Sally. She'll have to get used to living in a new place. She'll have a new school. She'll have to make new friends. And on top of that, she'll be grieving," Rachel said.

"You do understand." It was only proof the Lord had brought him here for a reason. He felt overwhelmed with his responsibilities toward Sally—not that he was about to let her down. He was all she had. "I want to do right by her. It's just gonna take a lot to help her through this."

"But she will get through it. She has you."

"I'm not going to be enough for her." Honesty. It popped off his tongue before he had a chance to think of a less-revealing answer. He felt exposed as Rachel turned on him her sympathetic gaze, as tender as a touch, and he reeled from it.

He wasn't comfortable being this close to anyone, and yet it was too late to take back the words. They could not be unspoken, and now he heard the silence between them. And he worried she would think the same thing. He didn't want this woman he liked—he really did—to think less of him.

"You're her uncle. You're a big strong warrior who has faced danger all over this world and put your life on the line for what was right. What better man to take care of a vulnerable child?"

He shook his head, as if he really thought she was wrong. "I know nothing about little girls. Not really. I hardly know Sally. I've been deployed most of her life. We're more strangers than family."

"I've seen you two together. I don't believe that."

"Then you're wrong." He didn't know how to explain it. He'd kept contact with Sally and his sister over the years, they were the only family he had since his parents' deaths. He'd loved Jeanette and his niece, but his career was beyond demanding, and he had little time for more than a phone call every few weeks.

He loved Sally. But it had been from a great distance.

He rescued soldiers who were in trouble wherever and whenever they needed him. He couldn't do that and be home to take care of Sally.

"If we're going to be friends, then there's one thing you'd better know about me right up front, Mr. Jake Hathaway."

"What's that?"

"I'm never wrong. Well, not about this. I know exactly what it's like to have your world shatter. But I was lucky. Paige was old enough to keep us together. To hang on to the diner and this house. She became the head of the family. Our uncle Pete kept a close watch on us, and he helped out always. But Paige kept us a family. She gave up her dreams of going to college to stay and raise us. To run the diner. To make the mortgage payments. To make sure we got through school and into college if we wanted."

"You went to college?"

"I'm a waitress with a bachelor in education and English. I wanted to teach."

"That's why you're so good with kids. You would have made a great teacher. Why didn't you?"

"That's tricky. It's about doing the right thing. I bet you know something about that."

Her gaze fastened on his. For all her softness she was a very direct woman. He could see the steel in her, too, a strength that made him sit up a little straighter and respect her. "Family," he guessed.

"Yes. Paige stayed to run the diner for us. And now that her son's a senior in high school, he'll be going away to college next year, Paige wants to get on with some of the goals she had to set aside. I've agreed to take over the diner for her. Which means I have to learn things like bookkeeping and purchasing and managing."

"When you'd rather be a teacher."

"I'd rather see my sister happy. She deserves it, after all she's done for me. For all of us."

Shame exploded in his chest. The Lord worked in mysterious ways, but He was always faithful. Always awesome.

Jake had been struggling with what to do—and the good Father had brought him here, to this woman of gentleness and goodness, to remind him of what really mattered in this life. Family. Keeping children safe. It was why he trained so hard and pushed himself so far every day he wore his uniform.

He believed in what he did—saving others, protecting others and defending this country so women like Rachel and children like Sally could live their lives in peace and safety.

Before he could turn to thank Rachel for her gentle reminders on this peaceful evening, the sliding door rasped open and there was Ben, walking with a slight limp, looking a ton better than he had the last time Jake had seen him in the field hospital. He chose to leave his thanks unspoken to Rachel and stood to greet his best friend.

Hours later in the hotel as he watched Sally sleep through the motel room's adjoining door, he remembered to give thanks for his time spent with Rachel. The thought of her stuck with him, like an imprint on his soul.

Chapter Five

There was something about weddings. A singular joy raced through Rachel's soul as she stood next to Cadence, her brother's soon-to-be-wife, in the crowded little room in the church's basement. She would be gaining a sister today.

"Of course it would have to be the windiest day ever." Cadence rolled her eyes in good humor despite the tangle of her once-perfect curls. "At least I look more like myself this way. Ben isn't used to seeing me all dressed up, instead of with my wet hair tied back after a day working at the pool."

Cadence was a swimming instructor and diving coach at the county pool, and her hair was wet and tied back in a ponytail more often than not. As the first of the autumn leaves scoured the basement window, Rachel handed Paige one of the homemade pearl-and-ribboned barrettes that perfectly matched Cadence's homemade wedding dress. Paige wielded the curling iron with skill before plucking the barrette from Rachel's fingers.

Weddings were like fairy tales coming true. Rachel couldn't hold back the happiness she felt for Cadence and her brother. They had found true love, one of God's greatest blessings. *Please, Father,* she prayed, *protect them and guide them. Help them to make their love stronger with every passing day.*

Rachel caught Cadence's gaze in the mirror. "You have never looked more lovely."

The bride's chin wobbled. "I've never been more nervous in my entire life. I'm getting married, not competing in the Olympics. But look at me." She held up her hand, lovely with a new manicure. "Like a leaf."

"Nerves are perfectly normal," Amy commented from the doorway behind them, where she was gently shaking out the beautiful tulle and pearl veil. "When I married Heath, I was scared to death. And it didn't make any sense because I wanted to be his wife more than anything."

"That's exactly how I feel." Cadence lowered her trembling hands to the edge of the dressing table and took a steadying breath. "I love your brother more than my life. But I'm not sure if I can keep my knees steady enough to walk down the aisle to marry him."

"You'll be fine." Paige slid the final barrette into

place in Cadence's thick, beautiful hair. "Once you see Ben, the nerves will slip away."

"Do you promise?"

"Absolutely."

"That isn't making me shake less." Cadence's chuckle was a nervous one.

Rachel took her trembling hands and squeezed. "It's an important moment and worthy of anxiety. You want it to go right. You want your life from this moment on to be full of love and happiness."

"I don't want to disappoint Ben. I love him so much."

Rachel melted, because this was the way love should be. The only kind of love she wanted for her friend Cadence and her brother, but also, one day, for herself.

"Oh! They're ready for us!" Amy exclaimed from the doorway. "Do you hear the organ upstairs?"

The first sweet strains of "Amazing Grace" sifted through the floorboards and the sound seemed to hearten Cadence. The beautiful bride managed a calm smile. "Ben is waiting for me?"

"He's at the top of the stairs," Amy answered as she carefully handed the veil to Paige.

Cadence's eyes teared. "This is it. I'm really going to get married."

"Really and truly." Rachel could feel the change as she helped Cadence to stand. "How are those wobbly knees?"

"Only a little shaky. I'm doing better. You're right. I

just need to see Ben and I'll be fine." The bride gasped as Paige secured the veil, and the delicate fabric fluttered over her beautiful face. "Do I really look all right? Do you think he'll be pleased?"

"He's going to burst with pride when he sees you." Paige leaned close to hug Cadence, and then stepped aside so Amy could do the same. "Welcome to the family."

Rachel swiped at her tears. Her friend glowed with a radiance that only a bride in love could have. She passed out the bouquets. The gentle fragrance of roses and lavender seemed to bless them as they filed out of the room and up the stairs where organ music filled the sanctuary. Amy's strapping husband Heath offered his wife his arm and led the way down the aisle.

It was so beautiful. Rachel savored the moment, her heart full as she watched her younger sister and her husband progress arm-in-arm. Maybe it was the glint of jeweled light through the stained-glass windows that seemed to bless them with a caring touch. Or the sweet strains of Pachelbel's famous canon began, and the music seemed to draw the couple closer. Amy tilted her head back, her dark-blond locks tumbling over her shoulders, to smile up at her man.

Big, solemn Heath met her gaze and for an instant it was as if the world stopped moving, the music stood still and the sunlight beaming from above brightened. The abiding love between wife and husband seemed to have a shine of its own. A beauty that added to the beauty in the church. Although the pews were mostly empty—Cadence and Ben wanted a small wedding—a collective sigh of awe seemed to whisper through the aisles.

Happiness wrapped around Rachel like a hug. The loneliness of her own personal life hardly mattered. Not when she saw how blessed Amy was. And how happy Cadence and Ben could be. One day, she would have joy like this. And until then, she gave thanks that the people she loved most had found what her heart yearned for. There was nothing more important on this earth than love.

"They look committed to one another." A familiar baritone rumbled next to her ear.

Rachel jumped. She hadn't heard anyone approach, but there was a man right beside her, tall and handsome in a black tux. "Jake. You scared me to death."

"Sorry. I'm trained to be stealthy. Didn't mean to sneak up on you."

"Well, you did. You're the dude I'm supposed to let escort me down the aisle."

"Yes ma'am, if you're the maid of honor."

"Guilty."

She took one look at his strong arm. Even beneath the black fabric she knew he would feel like tensed steel. The aisle stretched out ahead of them, and the idea of fitting her arm against his gave her a sudden jolt of panic. She didn't know why, and she couldn't explain it.

Before she'd met him, she knew she'd be walking down the aisle with Ben's best friend. But now that she'd met him and actually liked him, and seen that in that tuxedo he was the single most handsome man she'd ever seen, her heart flip-flopped in her chest and gave a romantic tumble all the way to her toes.

It wasn't love, of course. Love took time, it took commitment and careful tending. But this was a serious case of like. As she threaded her arm through his, she had to fight to keep her feet firmly on the ground. The solid feel of him, his steady presence at her side, the way his gait seemed to match hers, there was something right about being so close to him, like a key in a lock. Her heart clicked.

The sun chose that moment to beam even more brightly through the rich panels of the stained-glass windows, and it felt like heaven's touch cradling them in light and color. The church was a blur—the candles, the flowers and the faces of the guests standing as the wedding march began. But none of that seemed to register, not next to the absolute calm that came into her soul.

Jake released her and she realized they were at the altar where their beloved pastor was smiling kindly, his Bible in hand. Dazed, she took her place beside Amy, her vision too bright to see anything but Jake settling into place beside Heath, putting his hands behind his back and turning to face the bride and groom.

She felt changed and she didn't know why. She was still the same; she still felt the same, still thought the same. Everything around her was the same. But it was as if something had transformed; as if she'd taken a step in a fork in the road that she couldn't see, only feel.

"They are going to be so happy together," Amy leaned close to whisper. "Look at them."

The bride and groom glowed. Not in a flashy obvious way. But as they approached the altar, it was easy to see the deep steady light that filled them. The same light of an unshakable love that silenced everyone in the sanctuary.

I want a love like that, Rachel wished.

This time it didn't feel so far out of reach.

"Rachel."

The male voice coming from behind her in the diner didn't sound right, but she turned without thinking, Jake's name on the tip of her tongue. Even as she realized it wasn't the handsome best man who had approached her.

She took in the blond hair, the dark eyes and the familiar look to him. She didn't recognize him right off. "Wait. Derrick Whitley, right?"

"Yep, that's me." He strolled to a stop beneath the black and gold banner reading Congratulations! that swung over the aisle. He jammed his hands in his pockets. He'd matured, he'd put on a good thirty pounds, but he had a humble smile. "I don't know if you've heard, but I'm moving back to Montana."

"Your mom mentioned it to me the last time she was in the diner." Mrs. Whitley had also said that Derrick was an accountant who made a fine living and was single, since he'd divorced his unfaithful wife. It was hard not to feel sorry for Derrick. He still seemed as nice as ever. "Ben said you two have managed to stay friends."

"It's not easy keeping up with him. I hear he's going back to Florida after the honeymoon. And that Paige is leaving the diner to you."

"You know a lot for a man who's been out of town for the last decade or so."

"Mom keeps me updated." Derrick reached into his shirt pocket. "If you need help when you take over the diner, maybe you'll be looking for a new accountant. Give me a call. Or maybe I could just stop by and see you sometime. You know, during lunch."

"Sure." Not that she was so interested in Derrick, but this was more than a surprise. She couldn't shake the feeling that something had fundamentally changed in her life, in the path she was walking, and so she accepted the card with a nod and pointed Derrick in the direction of the buffet line.

Where had her nephew gone off to? She spun around, searching through the arriving guests for her favorite little boy. A little girl dressed in a purple sundress and matching lavender sandals gave a little wave from the front door.

"Rachel!" Sally hung on to her uncle's hand, all the trust in the world shining in her eyes as she clung to him. "I gotta grape dress, too!"

"We match." Rachel gave her full skirt a swish. "Do you want to come with me?"

"Um, okay." Sally tipped her head back, her full curls cascading over her reed-thin shoulders. "You're comin' too, huh, Uncle Jake?"

Rachel found it hard to keep her admiration volume on low as Jake gave a slow nod. She braced herself against that high-wattage smile of his, but he didn't smile. No dimples, nothing. Instead she saw the iron curve of his jaw. The hard gleam of his stormy eyes. And the military stance of a soldier at attention.

"Sure." Jake's lips barely moved. "Go ahead."

Was something wrong? The last time she'd seen him, he'd looked happy congratulating Ben after the ceremony. As Sally sidled up and reached for her hand, Rachel decided Jake had a lot on his mind. He carried serious responsibilities on those wide shoulders of his. She knew he was hoping to leave on a late-afternoon plane. "Did you want to help yourself to the buffet? I'll get Sally fed. Does that sound like a good plan?"

"It does." He didn't look at her but pushed up the sleeve of his jacket to study his watch. "We've got plenty of time. I made a call to the airline on the way over. As of five minutes ago, they have space available on their afternoon flight to L.A."

Okay, so he did have leaving on his mind. As she watched Sally press closer to her uncle, Rachel understood. The girl needed security. She was afraid of losing Jake, too. "Great, but I guess you won't be stopping by for that roast I promised you."

"That's too bad. Sal and I had a good time last night."

"Me, too." She didn't want to analyze that too much. He was leaving. Of course he was—she'd known that all along. It made no sense that she felt disappointed. "Hey, Sally. We've got a kids' party all set up on the patio. Do you want to come see?"

"Is Uncle Jake comin' too?" Endless hope rang in those words, and a child's honest need.

Jake let his sleeve slide back into place. "I'll come and see how you're doin'. You go have fun with Rachel."

"Oh. Okay." Sally swallowed hard. "Uh, when are you gonna come see?"

She thinks I'm mad at her, Jake realized and felt like a heel. "I'll come see you as soon as I get some grub. Deal?"

"Deal." Sally's eyes stayed wide and wary as she stuck to Rachel.

Rachel. Just looking at her made his temper want to erupt like a major volcano. He had to get a grip. He had to chill out. He was a highly trained soldier. He had discipline. Tons of discipline. So why couldn't he seem to calm down?

Good question. One he didn't have an answer for. He watched Rachel cast him an uncertain look, something between a grin and a look of relief, as she turned to lead Sally through the diner. The bridesmaid dress she wore was all soft-looking silk that flowed like a dream behind her. She was everything lovely and feminine and domestic, everything that was way out of his reach. He'd never felt turmoil about that before. He'd known long ago that his job and domestic tranquility weren't compatible. A settle-down kind of woman wasn't for him.

"Hey, Hathaway." Ben called above the crowd on the other side of the long buffet server. "Come meet Derrick. He jumps. We're talkin' about going up when I get back from our honeymoon. Are you still gonna be around?"

"What's that, three weeks?" Revved up at the thought of skydiving, Jake navigated around the small crowd at the end of the buffet. "I don't know how long my sister's estate is gonna take to wrap up, but maybe. Count me in, if I'm still on this side of the continent."

"Sweet. Jake, meet Derrick Whitley. We were in high school together. He used to have a crush on Rachel."

Derrick shook his head. "I did not. You don't have to go saying stuff like that."

Jake zeroed in on the civilian. He was lying. Flat-out lying. Jake didn't approve of dishonesty. Especially when he knew the man was just trying to save face.

Yeah, he'd seen how this Derrick dude looked at Rachel. Like he was looking at a dream come true.

She's not your dream, buddy. The harsh bolt of jealously zinged through him like lightning. His entire being shook from the force of it. Why? He wasn't jealous. He didn't let those dark emotions into his heart. So where did that come from?

He certainly wasn't getting into a froth over some stranger's interest in a woman, no matter how good and how pretty she was. It made no sense to feel so possessive of Rachel. He'd probably never see her again... okay, maybe once, if he came back to take Ben up on his offer to jump. But other than that...no way. He wasn't a settling-down kind of man.

"U-uncle Jake?" Sally's small voice trembled with uncertainty.

He melted at her big eyes. He could feel her sadness as if it were her own. Okay, he was going to be a settling-down kind of man after all. "Hey, cute stuff. Aren't you supposed to be with Rachel?"

A solemn nod. "She's real nice, but you said you were gonna come."

So much need. She stared up at him with a quiet question, one she didn't ask, and it was as if she were afraid he'd say no. That he wouldn't keep even the small promise of coming back to check on her. "Tell you what. You hang with me while I load up my plate, and we'll eat together. How's that?"

She nodded hard, relief easing the fear from her pixie face.

"Ben, let me know about the jump. Derrick, good to meet ya. I'll see you around later, Ben." Jake had a lot to talk to his good buddy about, but Sally was leaning against his knee, a steady presence that reminded him of what she needed. That was what his life was going to be. Making sure she got what she needed to get past her grief and move on. To be a normal, happy little girl again.

How was he going to do that if he had to leave her with a stranger?

His chest ached with sympathy for her. And love. He splayed the palm of his hand on the top of her downy head. "Let's steer you to the end of the line, cutie. You can help me figure out what to get. Do you want some of this?"

"Nope. There's gonna be cake, too. And ice cream, but we gotta wait for that. There's candies and nuts, though."

"Gotcha. We'll make a loop past the goodie table on the way out."

That suggestion went over with success. Sally hung close as he waded through the slow-moving line. The food smelled great. There was everything from barbecue to fancy sandwiches to a lasagna that looked like the most delicious thing ever. He loaded up on that, and a few juicy pieces of barbecue chicken. Made sure he got plenty of fries—homemade just like Rachel had fried up for him last night—and tartar to go with it. He added buttermilk biscuits and that delicious coleslaw.

He wasn't the only one loading up. The wedding had been a small event because Cadence was on a limited budget, but Paige was hosting the reception and had invited the entire town. More people kept streaming in through the door carrying gifts and good wishes. Folk called out to one another by first name and stood around talking as if they were good friends.

So this is normal life, he thought as he managed to crowd three big pieces of garlic bread onto his plate. This is how most people spend their lives. Everyone surrounding him was talking and laughing with one another. These were friendships and family bonds and community ties that he'd never given much thought to before. He never had the leisure time to stand around and think about it. He'd been too busy lobbing grenades and trying not to get killed.

Sally tugged on his jacket hem. "The candy's over this way."

"Lead on, princess. Where you go, I'll follow."

"They're pretty." She halted in front of the cloth-covered table where various glass bowls of nuts, mints and chocolate and colorful candy crammed the surface. Sally helped herself to a small paper plate and began to pick through the pastel mints. "The pink ones taste best."

"Then you'd best get a lot of 'em." He waited patiently—and he wasn't the most patient of men—while she scored a half dozen pink mints. The crowd swirled around them, the conversations crescendoed as even more folks arrived. Rachel popped through the open side door, where a patio was visible behind her, looking for children in the crowd. She didn't look his way.

Good. The image of her standing and innocently talking with that Derrick dude still made him mad. It didn't make sense. Feelings weren't logical. He didn't like them, he didn't trust them, and he never made decisions based on them. Cool logic, that was the best way to make decisions. And the truth was, he was leaving town in about an hour's time. If he did step foot in this town again, it wouldn't be with the express goal of dating Rachel McKaslin.

Chapter Six

Except for the fact that Jake was avoiding her, he had to be the most perfect guy. Rachel did her best to stay focused, but her gaze kept sliding to the back corner of the enclosed patio where he sat at a patio table with Sally at his side. Uncle and niece stayed in companionable silence as he downed his heaping plate and she picked apart her hamburger.

Amy poked her head through the doorway. "How's it going out here? Do you need anything? More root beer? More fries? Oh, and I left the box of stuff for the games on the bench by the front door. It looks like the kids are starting to get restless."

Rachel glanced at her sister and replied, "Yep. We're almost done here. I figure we'll run off some of that energy at the park and come back for cake and ice cream. Thank heaven for our cousin Kelly. She's been great with the kids."

"I'm glad she could help out. You look tired."

"Oh, thanks. Next you'll be commenting on the bags under my eyes."

"They're not *too* bad." Amy winked, so light-hearted these days. "You've been here since six getting all of this ready. Why don't you let me take over? Take a load off. You can put up your feet. Maybe grab a bite under the umbrella. Talk to a cute guy."

Oh, she knew exactly what Amy was thinking. And there was no way she was up to dealing with any of her sister's well-meaning matchmaking. It was best to ignore the amazing Jake Hathaway in the corner and play innocent. "What cute guy?"

"The best man. Did you know that Ben thinks he's great?"

"Like that's a secret. They're best friends."

"He's hard-working. Brave. A fine soldier. *And* he's totally available."

"Available for what? Have you forgotten that he lives in Florida?"

"So does Ben. And Cadence will, too, as soon as the two of them get her moved. The Florida thing isn't a major obstacle."

"Then what would be? It's clear across the country."

"Sure, but you've heard of airplanes, right? You could get on one and go down and visit. That way you could get to know Jake a little better. Let him fall in love with you a little more?"

"What?" Had she been so transparent? Did everyone know how she felt? Denial was always a reliable way to cope. "I don't know *what* you're talking about. I've got this diner. I have bookkeeping to learn. Paige is counting on me."

"You can study bookkeeping from a book. They have books in Florida. And what's one little visit? You work hard. You haven't had a vacation in forever."

"Vacation? That's the last thing I need." Rachel wasn't fooled one bit. Amy glowed with happiness; it was clear she loved being a wife and that Heath cherished her. That made all the difference in a woman's life. It made sense that Amy wanted that to happen for her.

But Jake wasn't for her. Couldn't everyone else see that? She wasn't going to open up her heart to the possibility. He was too good to be true, she was in serious like with him, and he kept avoiding her gaze. Probably because somewhere he'd overheard her sisters yakking on about how he was available and the poor man wasn't thrilled with the idea. "And it's the last thing Jake needs. He has his little niece to look after."

"And doesn't that just melt your heart? A big tough guy like him, he's so sweet with her. Don't you think?"

"Stop!" Laughing, Rachel held up her hands. "I give up. Just change the subject." She could never win when it came to her sisters. "I'm gonna set up a board game in case there are kids that don't feel like running around outside."

"So, you're taking me up on my offer?"

"Yep." Rachel spied a familiar little boy circling around the table to get to her. "How's my favorite astronaut today?"

"An astronomer, Aunt Rachel." Westin rolled his eyes in good humor, as if he'd given up trying to expect her to keep things straight. "Not an astronaut."

"Well, they both do space stuff. Are you ready to go run?"

"Yep." Fidgeting with boyish energy, Westin shot her a dimpled grin, designed to melt all of her resistance. "And then I can get a really big piece of cake? With lots of frosting?"

"No frosting for you. And only the smallest piece of cake. Go on, tell Kelly we're going across the street." Rachel grinned and ruffled the wild tufts of his cowlick.

She couldn't help the love filling her up for this little nephew of hers. She knew just how Jake felt. She could see Jake in her peripheral vision leaning over to swipe his last French fry through the plastic container of Sally's tartar sauce.

I'm gaping at him again. Embarrassed, she jump-started toward her cousin Kelly before Jake noticed she was sneaking peeks at him and got the wrong idea completely. The poor man. He probably got it all the time. Women probably fell at his feet in adoration. So she made sure to whisper as she sidled up to Kelly. "Tell me my sisters haven't been overheard trying to set me and Jake up."

"Okay, I won't." Kelly piled the last of the plates into the bus bin. "But they have."

"Great." No wonder Jake hadn't so much as looked her way! Her sisters were well-meaning, but they weren't helping. Ah, the joys of a close family. She rolled her eyes, unable to be really mad. "Go. I'll finish cleaning up. And don't forget to take Sally with you."

"Sure. I'll do you a favor and make sure her handsome uncle comes, too. I'll sacrifice myself just so you don't have to be around him if that'll help." Her eyes twinkled.

"Oh, that'll help. Thanks. Then my sisters can try to fix you and Jake up, and I'll be out of the loop." She liked that idea. "See how handsome he is?"

"But I thought you liked him."

"Like him, sure. Who wouldn't? But that's as far as it goes." Careful to keep her voice low, Rachel gathered the soda glasses from the table. The kids looked up at her with expectation. "I promised you milk shakes when you come back. Let me take your orders now. Allie, do you know what you want?"

"Strawberry!" Their little cousin sang with amazing cuteness.

"Okay, sweetie. You've got it. How about you, Anna?" she asked Allie's little sister and wasn't surprised when she wanted strawberry, too.

Rachel scribbled down orders as the kids started

shouting out what they wanted. They were loud and funny and she loved that they made her laugh. Just what she needed. By the time the kids were shoving through the doorway and out of sight, she felt much better and ready to tackle the next problem.

Sally was the only child left on the patio. Streamers waved from the open table umbrellas. Bright balloons floated, tethered by their colorful ribbons. The wind breezed through the trees behind the patio wall, and the afternoon sun cast a solemn shade over the girl and her uncle.

This is an easy fix, she realized. She had nothing to do with her sisters' schemes, and Jake was leaving in less than an hour for the airport. Easy. All she had to do was smile. The Lord would take care of the rest, as He always did.

"What kind of milk shake can I get you, Sally?" Rachel kept her order pad handy.

But instead of belting out her preference, the little one simply shrugged her slim shoulders and stared hard at the table in front of her.

Rachel tried again. "You look like a girl who likes strawberry."

"'Kay." She didn't sound enthused.

Jake stirred. "Maybe we ought to get ready to go, Sal."

The little girl sighed. "I don't wanna go back to California. I don't wanna go home anymore. It's not my home now." Her voice rose with high emotion, and there was no mistaking her dark pain on this bright, beautiful day.

Nothing could be more unfair, poor sweetheart. Rachel knelt, wishing she could take the little girl into her arms and hold her until the pain eased up a bit. But Jake was there, swinging Sally into his sheltering arms and bringing her to rest against the wide expanse of his dependable chest. She pressed hard against him, her little body shaking with silent sobs.

An equal sorrow darkened Jake's eyes as he met Rachel's gaze over Sally's soft, downy head. "Thanks for everything, Rachel, but I'm gonna take her home."

"Is there anything I can do? Just ask."

But Jake was already striding toward the door, and he didn't look back as he shook his head in reply. The broad line of his powerful shoulders looked invincible, as if he could handle anything. He could take care of Sally, she had no doubts about that. Emotion wedged so tightly in her throat, and she couldn't rightly say how much was for Sally or how much was for Jake.

One thing was sure, she wouldn't be seeing them again. Sadness punched her square in the chest, and it was a sadness that lingered and did not fade.

"I found an extra blanket, sir."

"Thanks." Jake took the folded blue blanket from the flight attendant.

Sally lay snuggled in the window seat beside him, her head propped up by two pillows. He'd given her his, and she was already draped with one blanket. But her hand felt cold against his arm, where she clutched his sleeve, even in her sleep.

He shook the second blanket over her and tucked it beneath her chin, careful not to wake her. She didn't move, nestled with her head in the pillows, her other hand curled beneath her cheek.

Tenderness for her roared to life inside his chest. She was so small and vulnerable. The memory of her sobbing so hard as she clung to him haunted him like a mistake. Maybe he shouldn't be taking her back to California. Maybe it wasn't the best decision, but he had no one to leave her with. He knew this was going to be hard for her.

Rachel McKaslin's words came back to him. *She will get through it. She has you.* If only he had Rachel's faith in himself. He would do his best, his very best, to be what Sally needed. Whatever the cost. But his best would be hard to give her when he was far away in Iraq.

Tragedies happened. He'd seen his share overseas, and here, too. He remembered what Rachel had said about her family's loss and her older sister's sacrifice.

Rachel McKaslin. He couldn't remember the last time a woman had disarmed him. From trying to rescue him from the moose with a broom to the absolute empathy on her face when he'd carried a sobbing child in his arms. There was no way Rachel could have known that Jeanette always made milk shakes or that the board game that had been sitting out in the corner, probably for the kids to play later at the reception, was Candy Land, a favorite game Sally used to play with her mom.

Sally sighed in her sleep and curled up more tightly into a ball. He watched her for a moment, making sure she wasn't about to start a nightmare—she'd been having them ever since he'd come to pick her up in foster care. She was so little. It was killing him. How could he find a nanny good enough for her? No matter what, he'd find the best one. *I'm going to make sure you're well taken care of, princess.*

A woman across the aisle caught his eye. "She's awful cute. I don't see a wedding ring, so are you a single father?"

She said that last part with a hopeful lift, and the bachelor in him balked. She was pretty enough and somewhere in her twenties. And definitely looking for a husband, for she had that certain intensity to her.

Too bad he wasn't interested, he thought, as he shook his head. Maybe he *ought* to be looking for a wife, for someone who could mother Sally. Help him raise her. Well, too bad he wasn't interested in marriage either, because it would be the perfect solution. "No," he told the woman. "I'm her uncle."

"Oh. You must be great with kids."

"Not really. Sally tolerates my incompetence," he quipped, looking away.

He wasn't interested. He didn't want this woman to think he was. He didn't want to be thinking about nannies or finding a quick, convenient wife. He wanted Sally to have her mom back. He wanted to be with his squad leading them through the desert on a search-and-rescue mission. He wanted to be back in Rachel's yard eating another Popsicle and watching her smile.

And where did that come from? It was out of the blue, that's what. And probably what he got from being so jet-lagged. He was starting to lose it. Just like back in the diner when he'd gotten bent out of shape because an old high-school friend of Ben's had been talking with Rachel.

And why did she keep popping into his thoughts? He was short on Z's, that's why, had been traveling too much. He needed some downtime, some sleep and to get back to his normal routine. He'd best keep up on his running. If he got out of shape, he'd be in a whole world of hurting when he got back to base. That's where his energy ought to be, on returning to duty and finding someone to care for Sally. That's it. No more thinking of Rachel and her slippers and her Popsicles and her sweet, endearing smile.

Tomorrow morning, he would have this all in perspective. And he'd have all thoughts of Rachel McKaslin out of his system.

It wasn't like he was going to be seeing her again anyway. He leaned back in his seat and closed his eyes. That thought should have given him comfort. So why did he feel more restless than before?

He didn't want to think about that too much. The plane lurched in a pocket of turbulence and the fasten seat belts light popped on. As the plane nosed earthward, climbing down from cruising altitude with the sprawl of Los Angeles in sight, he had enough to put all thoughts of Rachel out of his mind.

Three weeks and two days later, Rachel buried her face in her hands and made a long sound of frustration that echoed in the diner's small office. "Paige, I'm never gonna get this."

"Sure you will. You just have to concentrate."

"My gray matter is under way too much pressure. If I concentrate anymore, my brains are going to start spewing out of my ears."

"Well, I have a mop handy."

"Ha ha." What Rachel wanted to do was to run outside and keep going until she reached a land where there were no computers, no bookkeeping programs and no general ledgers she didn't understand anyway. "Derrick is back in town. He's a CPA. I could pay him to do this."

"With the little profit the diner makes, you can't afford to pay him."

"Maybe I can pay a bookkeeper then. They have bookkeeping services. They're listed in the Yellow Pages. I really think I should call or something. The good Lord clearly did not mean for me to handle accounting responsibilities or He would have given me even a smidgen of ability or something."

"It's not you, Rachel. Everyone feels this way about keeping their books. You just get used to it."

"I don't think I want to get used to this." Rachel didn't think Paige understood. How could she? Paige was smart and capable and she could do anything. "I've been trying to learn this stuff for the last six months. It's not sticking. I'm totally lost."

She smacked the endless and meaningless reams of printouts with the flat of her hand. It didn't help that she couldn't properly concentrate because her thoughts kept straying to a certain someone who was long gone and whom she wouldn't be able to see again. "None of this balances. None of it makes sense. You know you could still leave me the business, but you could teach Amy how to do this."

"But it will be your business. And what happens when Amy decides to stay home? Maybe she'll want to have another baby? Or go back to school. She has more options now that Heath is getting his state medical license."

"You're right. You're always right." Rachel loved Paige. She just wished she was more like her wonderful big sister. "I'm a failure. We have to admit it. There's no point in being nice about it. I'm doomed."

"I don't allow doom in my diner." Paige tried to lighten the mood.

But the alarm on Rachel's wristwatch gave a musical jingle saving her from more bookkeeping woes. "Oops, we'll have to continue this drama later. I've got to race over and pick up Westin from school. I promised Amy."

"And where is our illustrious sister? Isn't she supposed to be prepping in the kitchen?"

"Oh, I did most of that for her already. She got a call from the Realtor and she had to race over to look at this house that just came on the market. I'm so sorry, I have to go." Rachel decided to leave the papers where they were and grabbed her purse off the back of the tiny desk wedged into the hallway next to the diner's kitchen. "And my keys…?"

She spotted them on the counter and ran off before Paige could stop her. "I'll be back!"

"You'd better be. I'm not done torturing you!"

"Are you sure you want me to take over? When Alex graduates, you never know, you might be overcome with nostalgia and never leave this place. And then I'll have suffered the torture of computer work for nothing."

"Wishful thinking, little sister." Paige seemed to drift off into a daydream.

It was so uncharacteristic of her that Rachel couldn't

move. Paige had worked so hard over the years. Harder than any of them had in return. They hadn't needed to, because Paige was always there, carrying the load, shouldering all of the responsibilities without complaint. She solved every trouble before anyone even knew there was a problem.

Paige seemed to shake herself out of her thoughts, and wherever she'd gone in her mind, she looked happier. Younger.

Wow, she's really counting on leaving the diner.

Rachel breezed through the kitchen, where Dave, the evening cook, was prepping for supper, and banged through the back door and out into the chill of the early-winter afternoon. She shivered and realized she'd forgotten her jacket. She wasn't used to thinking summer was over, even when her sneakers crunched over the last of the amber and brown leaves carpeting the ground. Soon snow would be falling and the holidays would be here. Life went on, she knew, but she still found herself thinking of Jake.

Maybe she ought finally to accept Derrick's polite but persistent requests for a date. But the second she thought it, her stomach twisted with the simple truth. As nice as the accountant was, there wasn't that certain something. That special "wow" she so wanted.

Maybe she was too romantic. Maybe she had her hopes set too high? But if she didn't, then she would settle for less than true love. And that seemed sad, she thought as she opened her car door and dropped behind the wheel. The instant she sat down, a digital tune chimed from inside her purse. It was Paige, no doubt about it. Classic Paige.

Rachel unzipped her purse and fished around as the tune grew louder and the shaking continued. Where did it go? Oh, there, beneath her wallet and a roll of wild cherry candies. "Hey, what did I forget?"

It wasn't Paige's voice that answered, but her brother's. "Nothing that I know about. How are ya doin'?"

"You sound happy. Being married must suit you."

"What's not to like?" She'd never heard him sound so relaxed or so at peace. He was back from his honeymoon and a very happily married man. "Do you know where I can find Amy? I'm tryin' to track her down."

"Uh…you could try her cell." Rachel slammed the door and reached for her belt with one hand. "Or is she out of range?"

"That's why I'm calling you."

"What do you need?" She sorted through her keys and jammed the wrong one into the ignition. Of course it didn't fit, and so she had to shake through the key ring again until she found the right one.

"Jake's in town."

Jake's in town. "Nobody told me that."

"He's on his way back to Florida, but he's swinging by to help me load the moving van tomorrow, but I'm taking him jumping in about fifteen minutes."

"Jumping. As in out of a plane. Into thin air?"

"Sure. Piece of cake. Trouble is, if Amy's MIA, then we're staying grounded. Amy said she'd keep Sally for Jake."

Suddenly Amy's disappearance made sense. So, Amy knew all about Jake being in town and yet she hadn't said a thing cooking breakfast this morning. Now, wasn't it a coincidence that the moment Jake needed help, Amy had disappeared?

She loved her sisters, boy, did she, but she didn't need to give Jake any more reasons to run the other way. Her face was already hot.

Ben sounded mad. "Well, we were supposed to meet her here."

"Oh, are you at her house?" Rachel jammed the phone against her shoulder and maneuvered the gear-shift into Reverse. With the clutch going out, it was kind of tricky and she had to listen hard to hear Ben's answer over the grinding gears. She gave it some gas.

"No, cutie. I'm parked right behind you. Could you *stop?*"

What? She hit the brakes. She'd only backed up about two feet, but there was Paige's extra truck—Ben used it while he was in town, glinting in her rearview mirror behind her. She had a good two yards between her bumper and his, but still. Yikes! Did thinking about seeing Jake again have her rattled or what? "Sorry about that. What are you doing creeping up on a girl like that?

You know I've been banging my head against the wall trying to learn Paige's accounting system. I'm not right in the head."

"Sure, like that's news," he kidded fondly. "I have pity for you, really I do, but if Amy's gone, then who's picking up Westin?"

"Where do you think I'm going in such a hurry?"

"Oh, to get him from school. Cool. So, let me get this straight." She could just make out Ben's face through the glare of the truck's windshield but he was there alone. "You're going to be looking after Westin."

"Yep." Where was Jake? Maybe Ben was meeting him at the airport. That made sense. He wasn't actually going to be in town.

Ben kept talking, but a strange sound buzzed in her ears, making it impossible to hear more than distant gibberish as he began to explain something. Her attention had zeroed in on a movement in the passenger's-side mirror—there was a blur of color and that color became a man with amazing shoulders and a lean, athletic build. A man with dark, military short hair and an awesome presence that made her heart roll over and fall and keep falling.

Jake Hathaway was striding toward her passenger door like a soldier on a mission. Panic set in, but it was too late. He was already yanking open her door, already filling the space between them with a half frown and that intensity that made her stammer instead of speak like a normal person.

"Uh, well, h-hi." Smooth, Rache, real smooth. She gave a weak grin.

He didn't smile back.

Chapter Seven

"H-hi back," Jake stuttered, for his tongue seemed to be paralyzed. He couldn't believe that seeing Rachel again would be such a shock. Like jumping at twenty-five thousand feet where there was only icy atmosphere and empty vast air.

She seemed just as surprised to see him, as her lovely mouth was gaping like a fish out of water.

Yep, I know just how you feel. And that troubled him too because whatever this was, it affected both of them. That can't be good, he thought as he cleared his throat and tried to sound like a normal person. "Aren't you gonna come skydiving, too?"

"I'll keep my feet planted firmly on God's good soil, thank you very much. I'm not about to jump out of a perfectly good plane."

"Well, I just thought I'd offer. I appreciate you watching Sally for me."

"Go ahead and bring her in. I've got to run. School is over this exact minute. But Ben has my cell number, and I'll be out at the house. You can find me when you're done." There was only friendliness in her manner, and he wondered about that dude who'd been talking to her in the diner.

It wasn't his business if she was seeing someone and he wasn't about to lower his pride and ask Ben about it. Why would he? He wasn't interested in getting married. He was an independent sort and always would be, right? This deep awareness he felt for Rachel McKaslin would go away, right?

Sally nudged against his side. She'd climbed out of Ben's truck and was stalking him like a navy SEAL. "Uncle Jake, you won't make me stay with her, right?"

Okay, well, he wouldn't have to worry about this awareness he felt for Rachel because Sally was going to scare her away anyway. The girl had been getting steadily more clingy over the last few weeks. "Sweetie, I won't leave you for too long. I can't take you jumping with me."

"Oh." She couldn't hide her enormous disappointment.

Rachel came to the rescue. Somehow that didn't surprise him a bit. She flashed a winning smile their way. "Sally, you and I are going to have the most awesome time. I promise. Hop in."

"I guess." Sally's head sank forward in defeat.

Jake's chest gave a hard bump. The girl seemed like nothing but shadow. He'd done his best by her, but he couldn't blame her. Going back to California and facing memories of her old life had refreshed her grief. Maybe Sally needed Rachel's empathy today.

And he was grateful. "I can't thank you enough, Rachel."

"No thanks needed. I'm always happy to spend time with a good friend. Right, Sally?"

Sally didn't look as if she agreed but she climbed into the car and grabbed the buckle. Worry darkened her pretty eyes. "You'll be back for supper, right?"

"You won't have time to miss me much, I promise you that, darlin'." She'd been keeping close track of him, as if she were afraid of losing him, too.

Sally looked up at if she didn't believe him at all.

I'm not ever gonna abandon you, little girl. He couldn't help running his hand over the top of her head or the love that kept getting stronger for this child.

"Hey," Rachel broke through his thoughts. "I gotta scoot! Have jun fumping! I mean, fun jumping." She put the car in gear—forward this time—and he slammed the door shut.

The sedan cut through the long slant of sunshine and the stir of golden autumn leaves. His heart stirred, too, a strange mix of emotions he didn't want to acknowledge or name.

Jun fumping? Could she have bumbled that any worse? Rachel still wanted to wither up and die an hour later as she pulled into the garage with both kids tucked in the back seat.

It was too much to hope that Jake hadn't noticed. With any luck, she'd never have to see him again.

And hadn't she been in serious like with the man? Well, she might as well give up those thoughts now. What he must think of her, she couldn't guess, but chances were one hundred percent that he wanted to run in the opposite direction the next time he saw her.

Liking a man was a tricky thing—it was the first step on a path that made a girl way too vulnerable. As much as she wanted love and romance, a lovely wedding and a good marriage, she wanted it to be with the right man. That man wasn't Jake.

Rachel took a deep breath and tried to imagine the perfect man, if there could be one better than Jake. A man who would love her truly and cherish her forever, the same way she wanted to love him. The truth was, she wanted to love Jake. Her soul seemed to calm in his presence. This was simply another lost opportunity for true love.

She put the car in Park and turned off the engine. Westin's reflection in the rearview mirror caught her attention. He was already free from his buckles and clambering out of his seat. His hair was tousled and windblown from a busy day at school, but his energy not a bit dimmed. He bolted out of the back seat and gave the door a good slam, all before she had time to do more than pull her keys from the ignition and open her door. "Are you gonna be a gentleman and wait for us girls?"

"Well then, you gotta hurry." He grinned at her through the rolled-down window. "Cuz I'm hungry. What do ya got for me? Cupcakes?"

"Nope. Nothing but cold ashes for you."

"You can't eat ashes!" Westin laughed. "C'mon, Sally. Aunt Rachel probably's got cupcakes on the counter. You can have the first pick."

"Good boy." Rachel poked him in the stomach, just to hear him laugh again. Then she rummaged around for her purse, wherever it had gone to. "Sally, go ahead with Westin. I know I put it in here somewhere. Have you seen my purse?"

"Nope." Sally released her seat belt and dropped to her knees in the small space between the seat and the glove box. She looked under the seat. "It's not here."

"Thanks, I know it's here somewhere. I hope." This was what happened when she had tried to learn the modern torture known as bookkeeping. "I'll find it later. What I need more than my purse is chocolate. How about you?"

"'Kay." Sally managed a small smile. "Uncle Jake likes chocolate, too."

"Then we'll wrap up a few for you to take with you. Deal?"

"Deal!"

"Then let's go. Westin looks like he's gonna pop like a balloon if he has to wait another second for us." Rachel climbed out of the car, then ducked back in to grab her keys. Her nephew was holding the garage door, but was hopping up and down in place. "Why, thank you, sir. You're such a gentleman."

"My new dad says a man treats ladies real nice. Holdin' doors and stuff."

"A good man, your new dad, and you, too." Rachel waited for Sally and laid a hand on her shoulder to guide her through the doorway.

The girl was such a small thing, more shadow than substance, that Rachel's heart gave a hard wrench. She was clearly worried about something happening to Jake and being left alone again. *Well, maybe I can make the next few hours a little easier for the child to get through.*

"How about some chocolate milk to go with those cupcakes?" Rachel tossed her keys on the counter. Sunlight streaming through the windows made the kitchen cheerful and toasty and welcomed them over to the table. "Sally—" she gestured toward the chairs, "Go ahead and sit. Westin, grab the napkin holder for me, would you?"

"Can I have two cupcakes, no, three?"

The phone rang, saving her from answering. Westin already knew her answer—could she ever say no?—and she ruffled his head as she skirted past him to grab the receiver. "You guys decide if you wanna play a board game or go outside when you're done. Hello?"

"Hey, it's me." Her brother's voice warmed the line. "Got a question for you."

"First I've got one for you. Are you going to make sure your parachute is packed right before you jump?"

"Here, I'll let Jake answer that, since he's listening in."

There was the sound of male voices, a crackling sound as the phone was handed over, and Rachel didn't have time to swallow her panic before Jake's confident voice rang in her ear.

"I'm as safe as can be. We're about to go up, but I wanted to give you time to think about this." Jake's words dipped low and serious.

Rachel felt the impact deep in her soul. See how he affected her? No man had ever done this to her. How was she going to act normally, now? "What exactly are you going to ask?"

"Ben said he could use help moving on Wednesday, and since that's two days away, I can switch our flights, no problem, and stick around to help. But seeing as I don't make the big bucks, Ben suggested Sal and I could stay in the apartment. I wanted to make sure that was okay with you first. Say no if you're uncomfortable with a single old bachelor like me hanging around your house."

"The apartment's over the diner. Did Ben tell you that?"

"Ah, no, he didn't. Then I guess I ought to be calling your oldest sister. Isn't she in charge of the diner?'

"I'm taking over, and trust me, she won't mind if you stay. Ben could use the help, I know, it'll make this easier on him. And this way I get to spend more time with Sally."

Jake didn't miss the genuine affection in Rachel's words. He could just imagine her in that house of hers meant for a family, she was probably in the kitchen. Yep, he could hear the clink of dishes. The refrigerator door opened and his mind flashed back to the evening spent in her home in her company, and his world stopped spinning. Everything within him stilled. The back of his neck tingling like it did right before things got hot on a mission.

Except there was no danger, no enemies, no imminent ambush, no unseen threat. Just the pulse of his heartbeat and a strange stillness in the deepest part of him. It was as if God was letting him know that this woman was significant.

It was probably because Sally needed so much right now. Rachel, who'd known the same loss, maybe had the kindness to help Sally a little. Sure, his conscience scolded him, but Sally would be the only reason, right?

Right, he *wanted* to say. But he knew that was wrong. Sally wasn't the only reason. Jake didn't want to think about what that meant as Ben called out to him. The pilot and plane were ready and waiting. He said goodbye, hung up and took off down the tarmac, determined to keep nothing but blue skies on his mind.

Rachel heard the kitchen door open. The sound of boots hitting the floor told her two people were coming her way. She slid the dice across the coffee table to Westin as she rose from the floor. Ignoring the snap in her knee and the creak in her lower back, she ambled around the sectional, expecting to see Jake.

It wasn't Jake who strode into sight, but Amy and her handsome new husband. Heath did not look happy, and Amy appeared flushed either from upset or from a disagreement, Rachel couldn't tell which. But it couldn't bode well.

"What's up, guys?" Rachel left the excitement of the board game behind, knowing the kids were well occupied, and headed for the cupboards. "You look like you need chocolate."

"Chocolate's a start." Amy collapsed on the nearest chair. "No, please tell me these aren't your secret-recipe cupcakes because I can't eat just one. Heath, world wars could start over these, they're so good."

"The secret's in the filling." Rachel handed down two dessert plates. "Go ahead. Take as many as you want. They're only good when they're fresh. Want soda or chocolate milk to go with?"

"You shouldn't be waiting on us." Amy had dropped her purse, shrugged out of her coat and was unwrapping the paper from a cupcake. Chocolate crumbs tumbled everywhere. "But I love ya for it. We just looked at another house we couldn't afford."

"It wasn't affording the actual house," Heath added as he took a cake. "It was figuring out how to pay for the repairs it needed just to make it halfway livable."

"It's a tight market." Amy bit into her cupcake with a moan. She slumped against the chair back as she chewed. The chocolate seemed to be doing the trick. Amy already looked five times more relaxed.

"This is great, Rachel." Heath said around a bite of the crumbly goodness. "I feel better already."

Rachel poured two cups of cold milk and grabbed the chocolate syrup. With a few long squirts and a brief stint in the microwave, she had two cups of steaming goodness that made her sister smile. As she served the drinks, she thought she heard a car in the driveway, but it was the wind knocking the lilac bushes against the siding.

She had to stop thinking about Jake while she could. What she ought to be concentrating on was her sister, who had a real problem. Three people living in a single-wide trailer was do-able, sure, but it was a small trailer. Rachel knew that they needed something bigger, especially since they were hoping to add to their family. Not that Amy had said anything, but Rachel knew from the looks Heath and Amy had been sending to one another. They were so in love, so joyful, just so everything.

"I know of a house that would be perfect for you."

She couldn't help grabbing one of the cupcakes for her-self, not that her hips needed more padding than they already had. "This house I'm thinking of has four big bedrooms on the main floor, a roomy living room and this great country kitchen."

"No way. We're not arguing about this again."

"Not unless these cupcakes are included in the deal," Heath quipped before he took another healthy bite and said to Amy, "What? What's wrong with that?"

"That's an offer I'm gonna accept." Rachel ignored her sister, who was giving her new husband the narrow glare that all men learned to fear. "It's too late to back out. Your word is binding, Heath."

"Wow. And I was kidding about the cupcakes. We don't want your house, Rachel."

"Yeah, Rache, you've lived here nearly all your life." Amy abandoned her cupcake and caught Rachel's free hand with hers. "You deserve this place. I know what you're going to say, that this is where I grew up, too, but I left home, remember? I ran off and left you and Paige with the diner and when I came back, I didn't have the right to oust you. I still don't."

"This isn't about your feelings." Rachel couldn't be-lieve she sounded so irritated—and she *was* irritated. Because even as she tossed the cupcake wrapper in the garbage, she wanted to whack it upside her sister's head—not hard, of course—to make her see. "This place is too big for me."

"But you're happy here. You love the memories that are here. I'm not taking that from you. The right house for us will turn up."

"This *is* the right house." Couldn't anyone else see it? "This is a house for a family, and I don't have one of those."

"One day you will."

"Good, I would love nothing more, but one day isn't today. And today your family needs a larger place—this place. Look." She gestured to the window where a movement caught her eyes. Westin and Sally were leaping from the deck. "He's happy here. Look at him. Plus, there's already a swing set and the roof is good for another fifteen years."

One of these days, Amy was going to see reason. Until then, Rachel wasn't giving up her cause. She took a big bite and savored the rich fudge frosting and moist chocolate cake crumbling across her tongue. The secret whipped-cream filling was so sweet that it ought to make her forget her upset over the house and the fact that Jake was going to come breezing through that door anytime—

"Hey, do I rate enough to get one of those?"

His voice. Jake's voice. The pleasant rumble of it wrapped around her soul and squeezed. Unfortunately her mouth was full of cupcake, and the instant she locked her gaze on the fine sight of him, she automatically gasped. She felt a few crumbs being sucked down the wrong way and she fought hard not to start coughing. Too late. She covered her mouth and luckily the cough wasn't a big one. Tears filled her eyes and blurred her vision as she struggled to clear her throat.

Ben came to her rescue, amazing as always, as he strode straight to the table and stole two cupcakes. "Now this is what dessert tastes like in paradise. C'mon, take a bite." He tossed one to Jake who caught it with one hand. "Hey, Rachel."

She mumbled hello as she watched Jake catch the cupcake with one hand. Was it her imagination, or did he look more awesome than usual? His short dark hair was seriously windblown, and it seemed impossible that a man could look even better every time she saw him. And kinder, she added, when their gazes locked. "Did you guys have a good jump?"

"Yep, went up a couple a times. Good weather. Great views. I could see all the way to Yellowstone."

It took no effort at all to imagine him falling fearlessly with a packed chute on his back, the airplane above and the earth below. His cheeks were windburned and his inner spirit glowed from the exhilaration. It was as if the layers had been peeled away and she could see the true soul of this man—fearless and stalwart and unfailing.

Her heart gave a little tumble. Not that she was falling for him or anything, but it was hard not to like him more and more. And how could she help it? She took another bite of her cupcake, just to keep her jaw from sagging.

One brow hooked upward, as dashing as any silver-screen star's, Jake asked, "Did you bake these?"

Her mouth was full again, so she nodded, chewing fast and swallowing. "I've been known to dabble in the kitchen."

"Pretty fancy."

"Just the outside. Wait 'til you taste it."

He rose to her challenge and took a huge bite. He rolled his eyes as a sign of ecstasy.

"My own secret recipe." She couldn't help smiling wide. "I made two whole dozen, so have as many as you'd like. How about a plate to go with that?"

When he shook his head, she asked, "A napkin? A glass of chocolate milk?"

"I'm a fan of chocolate milk. Count me in," he said around a mouthful.

"One tall glass, coming up." She tossed him another smile before she made a U-turn toward the refrigerator. "How about you, Ben?"

He nodded as he took a big bite, his attention focused on dragging out a chair next to Amy. "Gonna sit, Jake?"

While Jake's pleasant baritone answered, and another chair scraped along the linoleum, Rachel plopped her half-eaten cupcake on a napkin and got to work. Glasses, plenty of chocolate syrup and cold milk. While she stirred each glass, she enjoyed the sounds of conversation: Ben and Heath talking about the real estate market, and Amy asking Jake if Sally knew how to swim and could she come along with her and Westin on their planned jaunt to one of the county pools.

That would be good for Sally, Rachel thought as she gave the milk a final stir. But what about the uncle? What did Jake have planned for tomorrow? None of your business, Rache. Just serve the milk.

A firm hand settled on her shoulder, and it didn't startle her. Although she hadn't heard him approach, she felt the zing of his presence, and her pulse thudded loudly in her ears.

"That sure does look good. You are amazing, Rachel."

"Me? Really? That seems like a pretty big compliment over chocolate milk." Rachel tried to resist falling in like with him a little more. "Oh, you could charm the moon to the earth. I've heard chocolate milk is the cure for false flattery. You're in luck." She handed him the closest glass. "Do you think you need two?"

"No, thanks. That wasn't false flattery. " His dimples flashed and made her knees weak. "I meant every word. You are amazing."

He walked away, leaving her smiling. He thought she was amazing? Jake Hathaway, Mr. Perfect and Wonderful, liked her? She couldn't believe it. It was all she could do not to shout joyfully and that's when she noticed her reflection in the side of the toaster. She had chocolate smeared on her teeth.

Yeah, she was awesome all right. If she didn't stop embarrassing herself in front of Jake, they really might have a chance.

Chapter Eight

Concentrate on your work, Rache. Before you drop the potatoes. In the diner's warm kitchen, Rachel made sure Mr. Brisbane's Southwestern Special had plenty of extra hashed browns, just the way he liked it. Work was tough this morning because she could not get Jake out of her thoughts. And when she wasn't thinking about Jake, she was fighting off the icky feel of embarrassment.

How could a guy as cool as Jake think of her as anything more than his friend's little sister? She certainly didn't act the part of the sophisticated classy woman. If only she could be more like Paige.

"Hear that man of yours is back in town again," Mr. Winkler commented as he made his way from the front door down the aisle.

"Uh, he's not my man."

"Oh, pardon. My mistake."

Mine, too. Rachel looked around at the diner. This wasn't how she pictured her life turning out, but she was content enough. Soon this place would be hers to run, and that was all right. Her dad had worked in this diner as a teenager and bought it on a risk when the owners were facing bankruptcy. There wasn't a lot of money to be made in a small-town diner, but her parents had done okay with good food, friendly service and hard work.

As she spotted Mr. Corey, another of their morning regulars, through the hand-off window and cracked two eggs—whites only due to his recent heart attack—on the grill, she could feel the memories of her dad standing right here, merrily calling out to the customers as he cooked. It was as if she could feel a little of that happiness, and it heartened her.

One day, she might find a man who could make her laugh, someone like her dad, someone strong and good and big enough to fill her world.

Mr. Winkler's sausages were perfect, browned and juicy, and she piled the links onto the plate, added toast and hit the bell. Leaving the plate beneath the warmer, she took a moment to slurp down another bracing swallow of coffee and, taking advantage of the lull, measured up pancake batter.

Jodi swept by to pin up an order on the wheel and grab Mr. Winkler's meal. "Hey, I got a request from a customer."

What customer? She hadn't noticed anyone else coming in, but then she didn't have her eyes glued to the front door either. "You know I'm here to please. What do I need to cook up special?"

"You'll have to take that up with the customer. Can she come back?"

"Sure thing." It had been a long time since she'd had someone talk to her in person. Probably someone on a special diet, which would be no problem at all. The door swung open and a little girl ambled in, squeezing her worn stuffed bunny in both arms. Sally. Did that mean Jake was here? But before she could think to look for him, she noticed the dark circles under the child's red, swollen eyes. Had she had a real tough night? "Sally, come on over here and give me a hug. Would that be okay?"

Sally nodded her head solemnly. She was stiff with hurt and fear—Rachel could feel it as she gave the girl a gentle hug, bunny and all. She added a deep prayer from her heart.

Help her, Father. She ached to smooth some of the stray wisps that had already escaped her turquoise barrettes. "What can I get special for you, sweet girl?"

"P-pancakes with smiles on them. They t-taste better that way."

"They sure do. I'll get to work on that right away." She stirred Mr. Corey's eggs, then drew a chair over from the corner. "Come stand here and coach me, okay?"

A single nod was Sally's only answer. She still clutched her stuffed rabbit and didn't let go as she climbed up to stand on the chair.

Rachel remembered standing in the same spot, at her dad's elbow while he cooked and whistled show tunes. It was a dear tug she felt on her heart as she plated Mr. Corey's meal and got a good look at what had to be Jake and Sally's order ticket on the wheel, although she couldn't see Jake seated at any of the booths along the front window. Thank goodness.

He was probably in back at one of the tables, she figured, safely out of sight. Which was a real good thing, since he had a certain effect on her, and her embarrassment over last night—and her teeth—remained. She sure knew how to make a great impression on this man—not!

"Do you want a smiley sunshine pancake too?" Rachel snatched the tongs and added a half dozen sausage links onto the grill. As they sizzled, she gestured toward the jumbo-sized cookie cutter. "Go ahead and grab that for me."

"'Kay." Timidly, Sally freed the cutter from the nearby hook and held it by one of its rays. "I used to help my mommy all the time."

"Then you're a seasoned cook's helper. Just what I need." Rachel grabbed the pitcher of fresh buttermilk batter. "Go ahead and put a couple of 'em down. How many pancakes do you want?"

Sally bit her lip as she debated. "Three."

"Then can you get two more cutters?"

Rachel kept an eye on Sally to make sure she didn't slip and scorch a fingertip while she poured out rounds of pancakes to fill Jake's Plentiful Pancake Combo and Sally's perfectly aligned sunshine smiles. "Can you tell me when those start to bubble?"

A tentative nod.

Well, at least she was doing better. Her rabbit had been sat on the edge of the counter, as if to keep a watch on the grill, too. The bell over the door jingled cheerily to announce more customers. The oven timer binged. After reminding Sally not to touch the grill, Rachel donned an oven mitt, stopped to turn the sausages and rescued the muffins, golden-topped and glazed with sugar. She popped the two dozen muffins onto the cooling rack.

"Um, bubbles."

Rachel grabbed the spatula. Perfect timing. "Let's get those turned, okay? Want to hold the plate for me?"

Another nod. Sally held steady the white plate Rachel handed her and in a moment she'd flipped the pancakes, let them sizzle and slid an egg onto the hot grill. While the whites bubbled, she stacked the pancakes for Jake and spread them across the plate for Sally.

It was pleasant being here like this with a little girl. Maybe one day she'd have her children here, the way she and her brother and sisters had stayed here in the mornings before school started. Wistful, Rachel tried not to pin so much on a future that hadn't happened yet, but it was hard.

"Hop down and come over here with me." There were the ghosts of memories again, good and dear ones, following her along the counter where it took only a few seconds to add juicy blue huckleberries for eyes and a sweep of strawberry jam for a wide smile on each sunshine. "Do you like strawberries?"

"Yep."

"Good, then we'll put them here, so each ray from the sun is a strawberry slice."

"My mommy used the white stuff."

"Whipped cream?"

"In the spray can."

"Well, I've got some right here."

There's a beautiful sight. Jake froze in the doorway, staring at the woman and child who were side by side. With their heads bent together, they didn't hear the swinging door sweep open, nor did Rachel notice that he was there. He didn't move a muscle as everything within him stilled.

Sunlight filtered through the open slat blinds and graced them with a soft golden haze that seemed like a sign from heaven. He'd have to be blind not to see the way Sally leaned close to Rachel, her little shoulders almost relaxed. Her grief seemed several shades less as she watched Rachel spray whipped cream on a bunch of pancakes.

"How about a nice big mustache on this one?"

"A big curly one," the girl encouraged, leaning in closer and planting her hands on the counter. As Rachel swirled the spray can, Sally watched, enchanted.

Jake was enchanted, too, but for entirely different reasons. That strange calm seeped through him, deeper than his heart and into his soul. *She's the one,* he thought, seeing God's plan for his life as clearly as the sunshine through the window. Rachel's voice reassured him like a soft summer wind moving over him. A feeling he'd never known before.

"Let's make this one a girl. We'll give her curls. Okay?"

Sally nodded, more animated than he'd seen her since her mom's death. There was hope. He could feel it taking root within him. He'd asked God for a solution, for things to work out for Sally's sake, and He had led them here, to Rachel, who had a loving heart and a kind enough nature to nurture a hurting child back to life. To Rachel, who'd experienced the same loss herself as a kid.

I know what I need to do. Goose bumps shivered down Jake's spine as he knew with certainty what he was to do. Sally needed this woman, and marriage was the answer.

The bell above the door chimed, drawing Rachel's attention. "Oh! Goodness. I've got to get back to the grill. Hold on, just a sec, Sally." Rachel set down the whipped cream can and leaped to save the food sizzling to a crisp. She was still so wrapped up she didn't see him.

Was she humming? He couldn't quite get the tune, but her smile was dazzling as she called out a greeting to whoever had entered, one of the regulars, as she deftly filled his order.

"I'll get your usual right on, Jim!" she called as she hit the bell. "Jodi, I'll take Sally back to her ta—"

She'd spotted him, and he felt the effects of her beautiful smile. "—table. Hi, Jake. I'll get his order, Jodi."

"No, I'll get it," he insisted and held out his hand. "C'mon, Sal. Let's let Rachel get back to work because we don't want the cook mad at us. Especially one so lovely."

She blushed prettily. "It's always good to compliment the cook. Now, go, out of my kitchen before I burn Jim's sausages." She reached for a mixing bowl and started stirring.

He took the image of her standing there, haloed in light, with him.

So far so good, Rachel thought as she plated the morning's special and added a side of hashed browns. Her hand kept shaking as she shoved the plate next to the other ready orders on the window ledge. Jake's words still affected her. He thought she was lovely?

The back door blew open and Paige charged in, briefcase slung over her shoulder, her arms full of ledgers.

"I'm sorry I'm so late. It's been one disaster after another."

"That's not fair. It's only seven in the morning."

"Exactly. I fear what the rest of the day is gonna bring." Paige marched through and disappeared down the short hallway. There was a thud as all the books she carried landed on the desk.

Knowing Paige hadn't had a chance to eat yet, Rachel plated her last order, a number seven for the town deputy, Frank, and carried it out to him. He was sitting near the door, the sports section of the morning paper on the table in front of him. As she slid his plate on the table, she glanced down the aisle, but no sign of Jake and Sally. They had to be seated around the corner. "How are you this morning, Frank?"

"No real complaints. As long as I can get another refill."

"You've got it." She bounded to the beverage station, where a fresh pot of coffee had just finished brewing. She grabbed the carafe and topped off Frank's cup. Taking advantage of the lull, she went in search of Paige in the office by going the long way around. Sure enough, she spied Jake and Sally in the back, next to the last window that looked out over the patio.

"Heard you're the next one in your family that's lookin' to marry." Mr. Winkler called out down the aisle. "Is that true?"

Did he have to say it so loudly? She felt bad the instant she thought that. Mr. Winkler wore hearing aids, so it wasn't his fault. But still. All the customers turned with interest. She felt Jake's piercing stare above all the others. Did she really want Mr. Amazing to know about her going-nowhere romantic life?

No way. She spun on her heel and backtracked to Mr. Winkler's table. "You should know better than to listen to rumors."

The kindly man brushed back his silver hair, as if to straighten himself up a bit. "Rumors? Why, missy, we've got a pool goin' as to how long it'll be before you got a second date with that fella."

Was it her imagination or could she feel everyone straining to hear her answer? She glanced around and Frank gave her a thumbs-up—apparently he was interested in her answer. Her cousin Kendra, across the aisle with her husband Cameron, didn't even bother to pretend she wasn't listening, and, worst of all, Jake was watching her over the rim of his coffee cup.

Her chest tightened as if an enormous boa constrictor had wrapped around her when she wasn't looking and was crushing her ribs. "No comment."

Embarrassed again, she thought as she took a fortifying deep breath and headed up to his table. Best to pretend nothing had happened, she thought. It was the only way she could face Jake.

He was smirking when she approached and set down his cup for her to refill it. "How's it going?"

"The usual torture and embarrassment, nothing new." She concentrated on pouring the coffee without disaster. "How were the pancakes, Sally?"

Sally looked up from a coloring book she must have brought down from the upstairs apartment. "I liked the blue eyes."

"Those were huckleberries. A local wild blueberry," she explained when Jake quirked his brow. "And that was our homemade strawberry jelly, by the way. Can I get you two anything else? Paige just came from the bakery. We've got fresh cinnamon rolls."

"I can't believe I'm gonna say this, but I want one of those."

"Coming right up. How did you two sleep last night?"

"It's a nice set-up you have up there." Jake tried to swallow the panic bubbling up from his guts. He'd faced ambushes, doomed rescue missions and prisoner-of-war camps and never had he felt this sudden urge to run. He was a man who faced live fire regularly and he would not flee from this. "Sally and I owe you dinner for a change. How about tonight?"

"Sorry, I'm working the dinner shift."

"Then we'll figure something out." He watched her walk away, an average woman in jeans and a blue T-shirt, with a ruffled apron tied at her waist, but somehow there wasn't anything average about Rachel McKaslin. Her rich chestnut hair was tied back at her nape, and her leggy gait was easy and relaxed. As she pushed through the swinging door, he heard the low notes of a song. She was humming.

A second date, huh? Well, maybe he'd give her one to remember. He checked his watch. *After* he helped Ben move their stuff out of their apartment.

Marriage. It wasn't something Jake had given a lot of thought to before this. Now it was all he could think about.

The image of Sally and Rachel side by side in the diner's kitchen, cradled in gentle sunlight, remained in his mind's eye like a sign from above that would not fade. As did the desperate look on Sally's sweet face when he'd left her with Ben's sister Amy and the feel of undisguised need as she'd clung to his hand as if to a life preserver. Yeah, he was giving the idea of marriage some serious thought.

"What's with you?" Ben asked from the downside of a huge bedroom-cabinet thingy. "Staring off in space, that's not normal. What are you doing, thinking of some pretty woman?"

How did a tough, fearless soldier admit to that? "Just wondering how you did it, man."

"Did what?"

"Tie the knot."

"That was the easiest part. Okay, I'm ready. Let's lift on three." Ben counted off and they heaved the heavy armoire around the corner of the bedroom door. "Hold it. We're gonna take out the wallboard."

Jake froze, holding his share of the load. "This isn't as heavy as that log we had to pack around during Indoc."

"What did that thing weigh, a thousand pounds? That doesn't mean it isn't still heavy, though. Okay, let's shimmy a little to the left."

"You got it." Jake gritted his teeth, maneuvering around the tight corner and into the relatively open area of the living room. "How's that injured leg holding up? Want me to take the lead?"

"My leg's sore, but a few more weeks and I'll be back in fighting shape." Ben blew out a breath as they lurched through the threshold, slowing down to clear the door frame, and then they were in the clear. The moving truck, with the lift down, was waiting.

"Being a married man must agree with you since that bullet wound's healed up just fine."

"I'm determined to get back to the front with you and the rest of our squad." There was a clatter as Ben backed onto the metal floor. The lift groaned beneath them.

"Ready?" Jake asked. His back complained, his knees smarted, but they let the enormous cabinet down without any smashed fingers or toes. "What does your new wife think about your heading right back overseas?"

"She understands that I'm TDY most of the time. It's just the job."

Jake knew some women started out feeling that way. They liked the idea of being supportive of their Special Forces husbands, but the reality was often different than they imagined. It was one thing to take care of all the demands of a home and family, another to deal with car problems and military paperwork that inevitably came up, not to mention the long stretches of lonely evenings and weekends. "She'll be all right handling everything on her own?"

"Are you kidding? Cadence won Olympic gold. If she can't handle it, then it can't be done. Not that I want to leave her for so long, but I know she'll be fine."

"You have a lot of belief in her."

"I married her, didn't I?" With a grin, Ben blushed, turning away to hop off the lift.

Love. It seemed like a risky state of being, more dangerous than tiptoeing through land-mined territory or fast-roping from a helicopter under fire. Those things he'd done and still did without pause. But love and feelings and opening his heart—well, it was a lot to consider.

Jake waited until the lift was done beeping and in place before he gave the armoire a shove. "I got this. You want to make sure there isn't anything else Cadence wants to fit inside this truck?"

"That would be an impossible mission, bud." Ben laughed. "I'll go check with my wife."

There was no mistaking the dip of emotion on that

final word, *wife,* and Jake figured that was a fine thing. He put some shoulder into the cabinet and shoved.

"Hey," Ben called from the sidewalk. "Why are you on the subject all of the sudden? Have you met someone?"

"You could say that." Jake gave a final Herculean push and the armoire skidded into place. Keeping his back turned, so his buddy wouldn't guess, he reached for a cord to tie down the furniture.

"Someone you met in the desert? Or back on base? In L.A?"

"Nope." He tightened the cord and gave it a good yank. Yep, it would hold firm.

"You haven't been in one place long enough to meet anyone else. Hold on—" He paused, as if either gearing up his anger or his disbelief. "It isn't anyone here, is it?"

And how did he answer that one? Rachel was his best friend's sister, and that was treading on dangerous ground, too. "Let's just say no other woman has affected me the way Rachel has." It was the truth, at least.

"Not Rachel."

"Rachel." The tying-down was done, so he turned and jammed his fists on his hips. "You got a problem with that?"

"As long as you're good to her, not a bit."

"Then there's no problem." He might not be a domesticated, settled-down type of man, but he believed in treating women right. How could anyone not be good to Rachel? She was so kind, sweet and endearingly funny. She was like coming home. It wouldn't be hard at all to be married to her.

"Hey, handsome." Ben's wife appeared with a medium-sized box in her arms. "This is the very last of it. Except for the cleaning stuff and the vacuum."

Jake watched, a little envious and a little awed, as Ben took the box handily and stopped to kiss his wife. There was no missing the bond between them; it was like an unalterable light shining from her eyes and into his. What they had was obviously real. It humbled even a man as cynical as him.

Happiness. Maybe it did exist. Maybe he could have something like that. He was grateful to the Lord for nudging him down this new path.

Chapter Nine

Rachel ignored the burning ache in her feet and the dull bite of pain in the small of her back. Another twelve-hour day so far and it wasn't over yet. She'd gone from cook to bookkeeper to waitress to hostess and back again and, unless her teenaged twin cousins held up their end of the duties, she'd be handling more of the hostessing.

"Here's your chicken fried steak, Nora." Rachel handed down the first plate, positioning it just so. "I had Dave add extra butter to the whipped potatoes, I know how you like that, and here's an extra basket of dinner rolls."

"You're a dear. The best rolls in town."

"Thank you, since I made them. And for you, Harold, our blue cheese New York steak with baked potato and homemade slow-cooked beans." She gave the plate a little twist as she set it down. "And extra glaze. I know you like it. Now, do you two need anything else?"

"You've thought of everything." Nora's face curved into a smile. "Is your brother's send-off party tomorrow morning?"

"Yep, bright and early. Enjoy your meal. I'll be back to check on you." Rachel checked the aisle—she'd have to make a pass with a few soda pitchers.

A movement outside the windows caught her attention. More customers, she figured, since the SUV was parked right near the door. The long rays of the setting sun sliced across the man, simply dressed in a navy sweatshirt and jeans, silhouetting him as he opened the passenger's-side door.

Jake. He must have finished helping Ben and Cadence pack for their move south. Ben had to report to duty next week.

Which reminded her. Jake was Florida bound, too. He'd be heading back to his base, back to his life, back to protecting and defending. Her heart gave an impossible wish—just a little one—but it was more of a dream than anything else. Those shoulders of his looked strong enough to carry any burden. And his chest. What would it be like to have the privilege of laying her cheek there? She knew that no place in this world would feel safer.

"Rachel!" Brandilyn darted down the aisle. "You've got a bunch of orders up. I'll grab some and help you catch up."

"Ooh, me too," chimed in her identical twin. "You're gonna, like, turn into me, Rache. Daydreamin', like, every second."

"I don't have time to daydream." A lot of responsibility was going to land square on her own shoulders soon and she had to be ready for it. This diner was her future, that was where her wishing energy ought to be instead of directed at a man who was impossible for so many reasons. Mostly because guys that great, that handsome, that cool, that awesome, looked right past a quiet girl like her. Maybe she was too simple in this world of technology and fancy degrees and exciting careers. She didn't know.

God knew what was best for her, she believed that with all her being. But sometimes…just sometimes…it would be something to have her most secret wish come true. Her secret dream man was too good to be true— sure, she knew that. But still, the image of him would always live in the deepest places of her heart and had taken root in her soul.

It's time to get back to reality, Rache. There were so many people who needed her for more coffee, to grab another ketchup bottle, to refill their sodas. This was her life and it was enough.

"I'll grab the pitchers and be right back," she promised Mr. Corey on her way by the table, hurrying to help the teenaged twins, who meant well but often brought disaster right along with them.

They were juggling the orders for the party of twelve in the back. Clearly a nightmare. One of them—Brianna—was about to lose an order of teriyaki chicken, and Brandilyn was going to drop all four plates she was struggling to keep level.

"Let me grab these!" Rachel rescued the teriyaki chicken and tucked it along her forearm, swiped a steaming plate of lasagna from Brandilyn and checked the orders—Krista Greenley's meal was short her substituted baked potato—and hollered through the window to Dave and juggled two more plates. "Let's get these served, ladies."

She led the way to the back, and as she passed the long row of windows, Jake filled her thoughts again. She'd managed to go a whole minute without thinking of him. The front bell chimed, and the cool evening breeze wafted down the aisle. It was probably him and Sally, come for their supper. As soon as she and the twins reached the table, she'd send Brandilyn back to seat them. The less she had to deal with Jake the better.

A dark color caught the corner of her vision—the navy of Jake's shirt. He was still outside. As she turned her head to see him more clearly, he disappeared behind the open passenger door, but only for a second. When he emerged, he held a sleeping Sally tenderly in his arms. The soft evening light bathed them in a gentle rosy light as Jake pressed a kiss to his little niece's forehead. She stirred, snuggling more deeply against him.

Rachel lost a little more of her heart. Just like that. At this rate, she wouldn't have any left.

"Uh, Rache." Brianna brushed by, as if heaven was reminding her what was important. "Do you know where these go?"

With some relief, she got back to concentrating on work, serving the meals and checking out the newcomers up front. "Krista, I'm sorry, your baked potato is on its way. I'll bring it with the rest of the orders. Jenna, here's your chicken teriyaki. And—" she whipped out a small bottle with her now-free hand "—a soy sauce."

She moved her way around the table so she could check the front of the restaurant, but Jake wasn't one of the customers waiting to be seated. He must have carried Sally up to bed. With promises to bring steak sauce and Krista's potato, she hurried through the swinging doors and thanked Dave for having Mrs. Edison's order boxed and sacked. After grabbing more condiment bottles, she set the ticket beside Brianna, who was now at the cash register and talking to herself as she rang it up.

"I put in an extra container of tartar," Rachel told her former teacher as she handed the boxed meal to the older lady. "Have a good evening, Mrs. Edison."

"Thank you, dear."

Jake charged into her thoughts again. As she bustled down the aisle, avoiding the party Brandilyn was currently seating, she wondered if he and Sally had had a chance to eat. She caught herself just in time. It's not your business, Rache. She wanted to tell herself that she'd show the same amount of concern for anyone who was staying in the upstairs apartment, but she knew that wasn't the truth.

"Your baked potato with extra sour cream." She presented the plate to a smiling Krista and then handed out the Cheeseburger Deluxe and Mom's Super Meat loaf. She produced a few different bottles of steak sauces and everyone was happy.

She handed off the fresh container of ketchup, grabbed a pitcher of soda and one of decaf and made the rounds. Made another to distribute more butter and a complimentary second order of fries for the deputy who was not only a loyal customer, but who always went beyond the call of duty for her sisters and their diner. Rachel then sent Brandilyn away from the cash register—she looked too befuddled while ringing up a family of four.

"Bus for me, would you?" she asked the teenager, who agreed cheerfully and hurried off, cracking her gum.

"Busy night?"

That familiar baritone had her toes curling. She handed over the Coreys' change, thanked them for coming and as they moved away from the counter, she saw Jake. His short hair was tousled, his sweatshirt rumpled, and yet he'd never looked more handsome. Maybe it was the remembered image of him holding the sleeping child so tenderly. Or the depth of affection in the parental kiss to her forehead. His strength and manliness was warrior-honed, and he had a heart like her father had had, that of a loving and good man.

"It's a home football-game night. It always keeps us on our toes." Rachel handed Brianna seven menus, and as the Sheridan family followed the teenager, she realized that was the end to the first rush. Everyone was seated, Paige must have come in the back because she was serving table four's meal. "We'll have a big push out the door in about twenty-five minutes, and then things will quiet down. How's Sally?"

"Exhausted. She hasn't been sleeping well, and I think spending the day with Amy's son, playing and swimming and whatever else they did, tired her out enough. She's out like a light."

"I saw you carrying her." Great, now she sounded like a stalker. "Through the windows." She gestured at the long row of glass reflecting the parked cars outside and the impending twilight.

He didn't seem to respond. "I don't want to leave her for long. Do you do takeout here?"

"Sure. Here's a menu." No more social blunders around this man, Rachel. "There isn't a phone upstairs, but did you want to take my cell? You can call the order in, and when it's ready, I'll send one of the twins up with your meal. That way you don't have to leave Sally alone."

"You'd do that?"

"For you. Sure." She realized what she'd said a second too late, and embarrassment burned her face. She did sound like a stalker or something, because now he was staring at her. The openness was gone. He stood like a granite statue, and did not look up from the menu he was studying. Not even when she took her cell from her pocket and set it on the edge of the counter.

It's just not meant to be. She knew it; she'd always known it. She stepped back, determined to keep her distance and what, if anything, was left of her dignity. "The number's on the front of the menu. Just give us a call."

"Thanks." His hand shot out and covered hers. She felt the warm comfort of his skin, the way his wide palm engulfed her hand. And in that moment, when his dark gaze found hers, she told herself it wasn't her future she saw. So why, when he left, did it feel as if he'd taken her destiny with him?

Jake hesitated at the bedroom door, looking back at his little niece. Sally was still fast asleep. Curled up on her side, bunched in a fetal position, so small and helpless.

He eased the bedroom door shut. The fierce need to protect her roared up in him, and he fisted his hands in frustration. What good was all his military training and all the specialized skills he'd learned to defend this country, when they couldn't do a single thing to rescue Sally from what was hurting her?

Grief wasn't something he could ambush or capture, fight off or beat down. He'd never felt so inadequate or lost, but he trusted the Lord to guide him through this, for Sally's sake. Because he couldn't do this alone.

He heard what he thought were footsteps on the outside stairs. When he'd called down his order, Rachel hadn't been the one to answer the phone. He knew she was busy—he'd seen how hard she was working and how crowded the restaurant was, so he didn't expect her to be on the other side of the door. But when she was, peace settled in his soul.

Definitely nice.

"Surprise." She spoke low, as if she expected Sally to be still napping and gestured with the huge sack she carried in both arms. "I told you there would be a lull. I hope you don't mind that I came. The twins are on break and I couldn't talk them into coming."

"It's okay."

"I brought the makings for hot chocolate. Enough for two, uh, in case you want some."

He could only stare because she blew him away. He'd never known anyone this thoughtful. She just kept wowing him. He stepped back, holding open the screen door for her. "Come in. Can I take that?"

"Oh, no."

"Then what do I owe you?"

"Nice try, but I don't want your money." She moved past him like poetry of beauty and grace.

His chest tugged hard in a painful, inexplicable way.

"I don't want a free meal." He pulled the door closed against the crisp evening winds. "That's not why I ordered from your place."

"So? You helped Ben, we help you." She moved through the half-lit room, circling the couch and disappearing through the kitchen door, and her gait tapped to a stop. The refrigerator door opened. "I'll just put the milk in here. And I wrapped up Sally's dinner, so all you need to do is take this out and pop it in the oven, preheated to three-fifty, for fifteen minutes, and it will be just right for her."

Jake watched as she set a foil packet in the refrigerator. Her cheese pizza from the kid's menu, he presumed, and it looked like a little more than a pizza. Rachel added a large container, the milk he guessed, and another covered plate.

"For dessert," she explained as she closed the door and folded the big sack she'd carried everything up in. "Did you want to eat in here or the living room? I could put this on a plate."

Okay, so maybe he wasn't in love with this woman, but he didn't really believe in love. And if the hard pang that settled dead center in his chest and throbbed like a bullet wound wasn't deep, serious-like, then he didn't know what was.

He *did* feel something for this woman, he could admit it. He admired her. God was right. She would be great for Sally. She was perfect, she was wonderful, she was a dream, and he couldn't speak like a normal, sane man when he was near her. So he managed to grunt and nod. Maybe he felt more than like for Rachel. He wasn't sure if he felt comfortable with that. He was a lone-wolf kind of guy.

She moved around the small, rather dusty kitchen as if she were at home. She brought down the plate and found silverware, and he just watched her work, humming a little.

"You really enjoy this, don't you?"

"Enjoy what? I noticed you had the TV on. I take it you want to eat in there?"

He nodded. There were some reruns of a family sitcom that had just come on. He got all of two channels with the rabbit ears on top of the decades-old set, and neither was as interesting as Rachel. "You wouldn't be able to stay for a few minutes, would you?"

"Oh, I wish. You have no idea." She blushed, as if she realized what she'd said. How much she revealed.

So, he wasn't alone in this attraction, or whatever it was he felt. The weight in his chest began to hurt and hope at the same time. It was hard to breathe. "You said there was a lull. And I'd like nothing more than to spend more time with you."

"It's a football night, and the game is about ready to start. You can see the stadium lights from here. In about five minutes the band is going to be warming up, and everyone is going to be leaving me. Paige's son is play-ing, so she's gotta be there. And the twins are that age where they don't want to miss anything. I'll be off un-til the game is over, and we'll get slammed again. I'll need to help out."

He felt her apology, it hung in the air like the faint dust; it seemed this apartment wasn't used very often. But the place wasn't as neglected as his courting skills. Courting was different than dating. The decision to court, well, now, he'd never exactly been in this posi-tion before. So, he was at a loss. "Maybe you'd want to come to the game with me and Sally?"

"Isn't she napping?"

"Uh, yeah, but we can eat here. Have you had din-ner yet? No? Well, Sally's bound to wake up sometime. When you on break and we can go on over. I haven't been to a football game for a couple of years. And be-sides, we'll be leaving for the base. I'd like to spend as much of the time I have left here with you."

What? Rachel *couldn't* have heard him right. Had he really said it, or was her mind just playing tricks on her? He wanted to spend his time here with her? A chunk of meteorite could hurtle down through the heavens, punch through the roof and strike her in the forehead and she wouldn't be more surprised.

Jake inched closer. "Would that be something you'd be interested in?"

"Uh…" She knew her mouth was hanging open.

Brilliant, Rache. She knew the capacity for speech had flown right out of her repertoire of social skills. The worst part of it was that she'd gone utterly paralyzed, in the middle of bending down to leave both his plate and his boxed meal on the coffee table, and she couldn't seem to make herself straighten up and act like a normal, sane person.

Jake didn't seem to notice as he bounded across the room, closing the distance in easy, powerful strides like the latent power of a panther stalking his prey.

He appeared taller from her bent-over position. He towered over her, his chuckle easy as he took the plate from her grip and set it on the table. "Does 'uh' mean yes or no?"

"Uh…" There she went again, in command of her verbal ability. "Yes. I'll just run down and, uh, finish up a few things."

"Bring up a meal. I'll wait."

"Uh, no. Don't wait. Your burger will get cold. I, uh, I'll be just a few minutes." Or had she said that already?

See, this is why you don't date a lot, Rachel. She was no dating genius, that was for sure. Was there such a thing as being date-impaired?

"Sounds great. I'll look forward to it."

"I'll, uh, look forward to it, too." His baritone dipped low and charming.

Were her toes curling? Sure enough, in the cramped quarters of her sneakers, her toes seemed to curl of their own volition. Somehow her feet carried her forward, but she didn't feel the floor because she was floating through the room.

Floating. As if that made any sense! She felt even more lost as she fumbled with the doorknob. She might as well be groping in the dark. Surely, Jake Hathaway wasn't The One. If he was, then why did he live across the country? Why would he be gone from her life before she even had the chance to get to know him?

She let the screen click shut behind her, careful not to let it slam shut and wake Sally. Twilight had lengthened until the shadows were dark and thick, and she welcomed the privacy of that darkness and the wintry wind that battered her hot face.

Why do I want him so much, Lord? It would be nothing at all to fall absolutely in love with him. To see herself in his kitchen, fixing his meals, picking up after Sally, keeping house and sharing his life.

You're just setting yourself up for heartbreak, you know that. She wasn't sophisticated and dazzling, cool and coy, flirty or confident. Men hardly noticed her. There was no way a rugged, man's man like Jake would see past her mousy appearance to the real woman she was—or was there?

The high-school band blared into life. Cheers rose up from the stadium. All those families huddled in the bleachers, bundled well against the cold night. All those people living lives that she could only dream of.

Jake was only being kind to her. She was his best buddy's sister, of course he'd be nice to her. That's all it is, Rache. Don't go seeing something that isn't there, she told herself firmly, protecting her heart well used to disappointment.

Jake needed a friend, that was all. And if there was one thing she was used to, it was that. She took a deep breath and hurried down the steps to the diner.

Chapter Ten

"This way." Jake's lips brushed her cheekbone, his breath warm and pleasant against her. "I see a couple of seats."

Rachel's soul shivered at his nearness. It was like a dream to feel the singular intimacy of being at his side. This big, strapping man who moved with agile caution—he was always scanning his surroundings, watching the people around them, and she could see the soldier in the man. Steely discipline and skill; he was a strong enough man to be gentle as he protected Sally from the bump of the milling crowd below the bleachers. Her heart fluttered more watching him lift Sally onto the top step, swinging her until a small grin cracked her solemn face.

"Where?" Rachel stood on tiptoe to try to look up into the stands, but she was short, always one of the banes of her existence, and she couldn't see over the heads of the people going up the steps in front of her.

"Up toward the middle," Jake answered, leaning close to be heard above the roar of the crowd as the home team apparently made a down. "See?"

She followed the line of his muscled arm, bulky with his winter coat, and saw the spot he meant. There was a patch of bench visible through the throng of families crammed together, cheering along with the cheerleaders or shouting out on their own. Okay, it would do, considering they were such latecomers. But it was a little spot, she and Jake would be pressed shoulder to shoulder, side to side, thigh to thigh.

She gulped. Maybe they should put Sally between them. Good idea. She took another step and the faces of the people on that bench came into clearer focus. Her blood iced. Her shoe missed the step. She recognized a face in the crowd—boy, did she. "Do you think we could sit somewhere else?" Anywhere else.

His hand settled on her back, between her shoulder blades, and his touch was a steady, amazing connection and ached as much as it soothed. The warmth of his hand, the outline of it, even through her heavy winter coat seemed to zing straight to her soul and settle. "We can sit anywhere you want, beautiful."

Did he know what he was doing to her? she wondered, as she tried to find the stair with her foot and succeeded. No, there was no way he could. She drew in a breath and hoped her voice would sound normal when she spoke, but it came out all strangled as if she was in the greatest agony. "Anywhere but next to my old boyfriend and his wife."

"Old boyfriend?" Surprise lit his voice, and Rachel turned in time to see his left brow arch upward. Sympathy flashed on his hard-chiseled face. "Now, how could any man be so dumb as not to want you?"

If only he didn't sound so sincere. If only her heart didn't warm in response. Her whole world shifted. The next step she took wouldn't have felt so monumental—something had changed, everything felt as if it changed, and yet nothing had. Like the moment in the church, she felt an odd calm seep into her soul.

It was this man. This man and the right things he said and the good things he did and how he made her feel deep inside. He was going to render her helpless. She was going to fall so hard in love with him there would be no recovery. No saving face, no shred of dignity she would have left when he took off for Florida and his exciting life as a para-rescueman. She would never be able to hide the strong, strident emotion blazing to life in her chest like a Fourth of July fireworks display.

"We can go somewhere else." His words, his breath, his lips grazed her cheek and made everything worse. And everything more clear.

The crowd blurred. The cheers and clash of the game faded. Even the brisk cold wind ebbed away until there was only the light in the center of her heart, coming to life and then flaming higher until it seemed to take over her entire being. She did not want to fall in love—one-sided again.

Jake's gloved hand caught hers and held on. "This way."

He's leaving for Florida, Rachel. She vowed to chant that over and over until she got it through her head that she was only doomed for disappointment again.

She was hardly aware of climbing through the stands, only of the dread of sitting close to him. And the thrill. Of settling onto the bench and the feel of his hand at her elbow, helping. Of the dependable strength of him as she sat squished against his side. This close, she could see the day's growth shadowing his granite jaw, but she had no right to lay her fingertips there, against the side of his jawbone and discover the texture of his day's whiskers.

"Rachel!" a voice called through the crowd.

She recognized her friend a few rows down, sitting with her family. "Margaret. How did Kaylie's teacher's conference go?"

"It was a disaster. She's in so much trouble." Margaret's kind eyes said otherwise. "Wait until motherhood happens to you, and you'll—oh." She gave Jake a second look. "Isn't that Ben's best man? His buddy from the army?"

"Air force," Jake started to correct her, but bit his

tongue. Not his conversation. Rachel was already doing it for him, explaining that he and Ben served together.

Margaret, a pleasant-faced woman with really frizzy hair, gave him an approving look. "So, how long have you two been together?"

"Oh, we're not together." Rachel blushed, and it was a pretty sight. She dipped her chin, and the crowd began to roar as a huddle on the field broke up. The woman turned to family talk, Margaret had a couple of kids that Rachel was asking after.

He listened with half an ear; he didn't want to eavesdrop, but there was no way he could ignore their conversation entirely because he was pressed so close to Rachel. Which wasn't a bad thing. Her cinnamon scent kept tickling his nose and he had to fight the need to put his arm around her and draw her close, just to see what it felt like; just to see if it felt *right*.

"I'll see you at choir practice, okay?" Rachel finished her conversation, exchanged parting smiles with her friend, and then turned to him. "Margaret and I are both sopranos in the church choir, if you can believe they let me sing. We've been friends since we were in preschool."

She was pure sweetness when she smiled, and he could picture her singing in church. He already knew she was a faithful woman; and faith was important to him. "The church I go to when I'm at home has a great choir."

"Really? Is it a big church?"

"It's probably bigger than yours here." He'd seen the town church, prominent on a quieter corner past the park, and its high steeple and white siding spoke of traditional values. "It's a more modern place, but that has a lot of advantages." He waited.

"It sounds wonderful. I lived in Seattle for a while, when I went to the University of Washington, and I attended this great church with a fantastic choir. I love music. Of course, our little town has nothing like that, but it makes up for it in a thousand other ways. It's the people in my life who matter most."

"That's how I feel." It blew him away like a bullet to the chest. "That's why I do what I do."

"You have a very demanding job. A man has to be very motivated to do it."

One thing he was good at was motivation, and at setting a goal and sticking with it until it was achieved. If he'd had any doubts about God's plan, it would be at this moment. Anyone could see Rachel was happy here. The crowd roared, Sally's hand crept into his, and he turned to her. "What is it, cutie?"

"I gotta go to the bathroom." She looked so pale in the bright light from the dozen floodlights blazing across the field, that he could see every freckle blanketing her nose and cheekbones.

His iron-hard heart wrenched; he hated seeing her so unhappy. At that moment he felt the incredible warmth of Rachel leaning against him to speak with Sally, and it was such a range of emotion he felt. He wasn't used to this; he was overwhelmed. It was as if he went deaf, for he couldn't even hear the crowd's wild cheers at an interception. That stillness washed over him like the ocean when he was on a night dive. The rush of water rising up over him as he plummeted downward from his jump. The blades of the chopper silenced, the view of his buddies gone, and he was alone and sinking.

"C'mon, Sally," he heard Rachel say, holding out her gloved hand across his chest. "I'll take you. And on the way back, let's get a good look at the concession stand, okay? That way we know what to make your uncle buy you."

"'Kay." Sally seemed to like the idea as she bolted up and grasped Rachel's hand like a lifeline. "Bye, Uncle Jake."

Rachel McKaslin laughed down at him as she took a side step to make her way through the packed bleacher row to the aisle. She held Sally's hand and guided her over the obstacles of feet and purses and stadium blankets like a natural. Of course, she had a nephew she spent time with, so she was used to taking care of a kid. She was perfect. So, why wasn't she married? Was it because she didn't want to be?

She paused midway to the aisle to speak with a woman who looked to be about her same age in the next row back. Jake lived for football, he wouldn't mind watching the game, but so far he hadn't watched a single play. Rachel drew his attention and held it, and he couldn't explain why.

As the women exchanged pleasantries, he noticed how Rachel lit up, subtle as a twilight star, as she spoke with another friend. Here he sat in the freezing cold with his heart feeling like it was on the outside instead of safely tucked in his chest. He didn't like feeling vulnerable. For all he knew, Rachel wanted nothing more than a life here, with her family and friends, working in the diner alongside her sisters.

But You wouldn't steer me wrong, right, God? He thought of what was at stake. Sally, who clung to Rachel's hand and began to fidget. Rachel noticed right away, laughingly said goodbye to her friend, and then she and Sally made it to the aisle, where they descended the steps. Like a good mother would, Rachel kept a steady hold of Sally's hand and helped her down the wide, steep stairs.

He straightened, trying to keep Rachel in his sight, and it wasn't because she looked adorable and attractive and amazing even in a bulky blue parka and wash-worn jeans. Her lustrous chestnut-colored hair bounced around her face and shoulders. His heart seemed to drag after her, and that made no sense at all.

He was a tough soldier. He could handle being ambushed and cornered, facing it with the steel he'd been given from the Lord.

But he didn't do love, and he didn't know how to draw back the tenderness that made it feel as if she had taken possession of some vital place in his heart. He only knew he had to be careful.

What happened next was in God's hands, he knew, as everything was; but he also knew that the Lord helped those who helped themselves and he wanted to help Sally. He didn't need anyone—not really.

Sally did.

"Another licorice whip?"

Rachel accepted the offered red rope with thanks. "I have a sweet tooth."

"I noticed." He didn't seem to think her weakness for candy was a fault. "I've never known a woman who liked licorice so much."

"It's a sign of great character. Just like a man who can eat a hot dog after having a huge deluxe burger and an extra order of fries."

"I indulge when I can. A month from now, I'll probably be scarfing down an MRE and falling to sleep with my M-4."

"I gave up my machine gun for a cup of cocoa and an electric blanket. They kept me warmer." She liked that she made him laugh. The warmth of his chuckle filled her. "No electric blankets where you go?"

"No, and the desert can get chilly at night."

"And lonely, I bet." She sighed. She knew something about that. She focused on the field glimmering beneath the floodlights like a giant rectangular emerald. The suited-up high-school kids were grim during the last four minutes left on the clock. They were ahead by a field goal, but they'd lost the down. One slip and they could lose the game.

On the field, her nephew Alex, so tall and grown-up, gave his face mask a yank, concentrating, as the players lined up, ready to scrimmage. Cheers rose, the band sent a musical challenge, which the crowd picked up on, and the excitement in the stands rose to a crescendo.

All around her were friends and acquaintances, people she'd known all her life. People with families of their own, her friends married with their own children. They were happy and seated beside their husbands. It was wrong to be envious, because she wasn't truly. But she so wanted a life like theirs.

And this man, who saw her as a friend, was on the edge of capturing her heart. And she couldn't let him. She had to be strong. She had to fight against it as hard as she could.

Wasn't it just her luck that when she'd found the right man she could love, he wasn't in love with her? It was her usual pattern. Nothing surprising about that. Not one thing.

It's almost over, she thought as the visiting team's center hiked the ball, and the quarterback stepped back to pass. The clock was counting down, the home team charged and the quarterback went down before he could throw. Sacked! The game was won, although a full minute stood on the big scoreboard.

Cheers exploded full volume. People leaped to their feet, the band screeched to life, and the cheerleaders hurled their pompoms. The game was as good as over. For her, it was.

"This is where I leave you." She leaned close so he could hear her over the fray and couldn't help noticing how pleasant he smelled, of spice and man and the night. "I have to get to the diner before these people do."

"Then we're coming with you."

"But—"

"No buts. We're not going to let you go off alone." He plucked Sally from the bench beside him and swung her into his arms. "Right, Sal?"

The girl nodded on cue, sleepy-eyed, the last five inches of a thick red licorice rope dangling from her fist. She yawned and laid her cheek against Jake's sturdy shoulder.

Jake smiled, always a dazzling experience. "This is a date. I'm not about to bail on you because you have responsibilities."

This is a date? Her mind skidded to a halt. She could only gape up at him in her best fish-out-of-water imitation. This can't be a date. I'm in my work clothes. My hair's a mess.

Jake's free hand lit on the back of her neck. Even

through the thick parka, she could feel the warmth of his hand like a brand. A slow trickle of joy flowed into her; it was all that she would allow. Okay, if this was a date, then it was a casual one. An impromptu one. Last-minute. It didn't mean anything. She'd do best not to read too much into it, even if she wanted to. Getting her hopes up scared her. They were bound to come crashing down.

As she excused her way down the row, Jake stayed right behind her. His hand remained on her nape and didn't leave, as if he were determined to maintain some sort of tie between them. When she reached the bottom of the stands, Jake moved to protect her from the shuffle and bump of the crowd, striding easily and predatorily and in control. It was easy to see the soldier in him, strong and tough, and she couldn't help thinking, *Wow.*

Finally they were through the gate and out into the open street behind the school grounds. The street curbs were jammed on either side with overflow parking from the school, but the two of them were alone. It felt like a special night, Rachel thought as she watched the tall leafless maples reach their black, frosty limbs high toward the black sky, so silent and still. The tidy residential street was quiet, too, as they passed Craftsman-style homes with their curtains closed and windows glowing from the lights within.

So, this was a date. She'd never quite had one like this before, especially a first date. But as they walked companionably along the street toward the park, she thought it might be the best first date she'd ever been on. There was something right about walking at his side. Something real about the silence that lingered gently between them. She felt comfortable. She felt complete. *Is he the one, Lord? Please, send me a sign, so I don't mess this up.*

"She's asleep." He spoke low, hardly louder than the night, leaning closer still.

Sally was slumped, carefully cradled, against his chest and shoulder, her weight easily secured in his strong arms. She was as relaxed as a rag doll. What a safe place to be, Rachel thought. "Maybe tonight she'll sleep better."

"I sure hope so."

They were at the street corner, and the unlit expanse of road showed there wasn't any reason to check for traffic. They stepped off the curb together, in synch. Their breaths rose in misty clouds at the same time and place as if they were made to be together.

"So, tell me," Jake broke the silence. "Why don't you have a husband and a family to fill that big house of yours?"

She tripped on her own feet. Real graceful, Rache. She caught herself before she could do more than stumble, but her mind couldn't stop tumbling over his words. Was he making pleasant conversation, or was there more to his question? "Because I'm waiting for God to send me the very best man."

"You're beautiful and smart and funny—"

"Because I trip over my own feet, you mean? Or wear those huge fuzzy slippers?"

"Yeah, and chase a spoiled wild moose with a broom. You're a great cook, you help run a business, everyone who knows you thinks you're the sweetest woman ever. Including me."

"Really? Wow, I'm glad I've deceived you so much. I'm not all that sweet. I can be feisty and difficult. Just ask Paige."

He knew what he saw. He spent his life fighting evil men who would harm the innocent in other people's countries to defend his own. He knew goodness when he saw it, and he loved her for it. For the humbling way she waved off the truth like a shrug of her slender shoulders. For the kindness she'd shown Sally. For the peace just being with her brought to his war-battered soul.

He needed her. He could see now why Ben had married. Being a lone wolf had its benefits. He worked most of the year in dangerous places, it was his call of duty. But when he was home, it would be something to have a real home, to have her at his side just to talk to, to walk beside, to share a quiet evening with. Those were the real things in life, the moments that mattered, and how he felt had nothing to do with needing someone for Sally or any single influence outside of his heart. Rachel made him feel taller and stronger, more vulnerable and afraid at the same exact moment. "So, you'd like to be married like your friends I saw at the game. You just haven't been asked by the very best man yet."

"Well, yes, if you want to put it that way. That's implying the best man is out there somewhere."

"Maybe he's closer than you think."

What did that mean? What was he saying? Rachel gave thanks that she still had the wherewithal to remember to lift her feet high enough to step over the railroad ties that marked the edge of the city park. Maybe he wasn't talking about himself being the best man. Maybe he was trying to be encouraging. "I can hope so. So, now it's your turn. Why aren't you married?"

"It's hard to find the right person. You know how it is."

"I do." She sighed, disappointment sifting through her like the cold air through her parka. She'd been right—he was making conversation, not trying to tell her that he was her best man. She took a slow breath, finding her dignity. There was no reason he needed to know that she was hurting. "It feels impossible to find that one person that lights you up inside and shares your values and your faith and wants the same things from life."

"Yep. Aside from being compatible and loyal and good."

"Exactly. That's why I'm still solo."

"So, you'd like to get married one day. Maybe have a couple of kids."

"Definitely." Rachel felt something brush her cheekbone. It was featherlight and cold. A snowflake. She tipped her head to stare up at the sky and dots of white tumbled toward her, falling as if sent from heaven. "I suppose it's not very modern of me, but I'm an old-fashioned girl. I've always wanted to have a good marriage and a happy family. Maybe because I lost my folks when I was young. It's been elusive. But maybe it won't always be that way." God willing.

"Good. I'm glad I'm not wasting time." Jake stopped in the middle of the grassy park and cupped her chin with his free hand. His gaze was unreadable; his face was set as if in stone.

Wasting time? What did that mean? Her mind began to swirl like the snowflakes as a light wind hit them. She realized as he leaned ever closer that he was speaking about her. About him. Incredibly, his lips slanted over hers in a tender brush. Their first kiss. Quiet, sweet joy filled her heart unbroken, until he lifted his mouth from hers.

Her future shone in his eyes as he gazed down at her, solemnly, for she knew that he felt this, too.

She didn't know how long they stood together, with Sally asleep on Jake's shoulder, gazing into one another's eyes. The distant blare of car horns and the shrill shrieks and cheers of teenagers rejoicing came distantly, and hardly important at all.

"Guess the game's over." Jake spoke first. "We'd

better get you to the diner. Judging by the sounds of things, it's gonna be busy."

Like a dream, he took her hand.

It's a sign, she thought as she twined her fingers with his. Snow was falling everywhere, frosting the world as if making it new. She remembered to thank the Lord as she let Jake lead her through the storm and the dark.

Chapter Eleven

Jake sipped his second cup of decaf and watched Rachel over the rim. He'd chosen this booth and this seat on purpose because he could see her through the order window. And every time he saw her, he remembered the gentleness of her kiss. The scent of her perfume clung to him, cinnamon and wholesome. He couldn't stop the tenderness building within him; and it was that tenderness that scared him. It would make him vulnerable if he let it. He wasn't a man to give up control.

"Aw, she's such a cutie."

Jake hadn't noticed one of the teenage girls approach the table, but there she was with a carafe and chomping her gum. She topped off his cup. "Hey, if you, like, ever need someone to babysit, you should call me."

"Or me," chimed her twin who bustled down the

aisle with a plate of French fries. "So you could, like, go out with Rachel again. I mean, if you wanna date her."

"Which you should totally do, because there's no one nicer than Rachel. She's, like, way cool."

"Do you like her?"

Jake looked up at the girls and tried to remember being a teenager. It was too long ago, and he felt his age as he reached for the sugar canister. "If you're serious about babysitting, I'll take you up on it."

"Great," they said in unison, with identical grins, before breaking up and going separate ways.

"What do you think, Sal? Is it about time to take you upstairs?"

His niece gave a big yawn. "Do I hafta see Rachel first?"

"She looks pretty busy in the kitchen. You like her, don't you?"

"I guess." She didn't sound too enthusiastic. "Oh, she's coming."

How did he miss that? Sure enough, when he looked up, there she was breezing toward him. The tender ache in his chest, the one he'd better figure out how to control, sharpened as she drew near.

"I brought you another cup." She slipped a big mug onto the table in front of Sally, blushing as if she were remembering their kiss.

Sal took one look at the mug frothing with whipped

cream and drizzled with chocolate syrup. "Thanks. I guess."

"Good. I aim to please." Rachel's unguarded spirit shone for one brief moment as she gazed on the child.

He would love her forever, just for that. For caring so much for Sally.

"Is there anything else I can get you two?"

"You're always doing for us. What about you?"

"Me? I work here. I'm supposed to cook and wait on people."

"That's not what I meant." Jake, being a man of action, knew exactly what he had to do. "It's nearly eleven. Isn't that when you close?"

"Lock the doors, yes. But there's work enough to keep me here for another hour at least. Why? You're welcome to stay here as long as you want, but Sally, you're looking droopy."

Was it his imagination or was Rachel avoiding his gaze? He patted the seat next to him. "Sit down here for a second."

"I, uh—" Her eyes sparkling with humor, she glanced down the aisles at the half dozen full tables where groups of teenagers munched on fries and slurped down milk shakes. "Why should I sit down? Maybe you have a complaint for the manager?"

"Yeah. I do, so you'd best sit on down here and listen up."

Oh, he looked like trouble itself as he laid his arm

along the back of the booth, waiting for her to slip in beside him. How could she refuse? She still tingled as if filled with the gentlest light, and all from his single kiss. She obliged him and it felt wonderful as his arm hooked over her shoulders. She felt whole, as if she were made to be at his side. "Was there something wrong with your order?"

"*You* didn't serve it to us."

"That's because I was in the kitchen."

"Come closer." He pulled her so they were practically hugging. It was wonderful to lay her head on his shoulder and just to be.

So this is what it's like to truly come home, she thought with a contented sigh. The silence in her deepened as his arms came around her and his chin pressed against the top of her head. She was right. No place could feel safer than being in Jake's arms.

"How much more do you have left to do?" His question vibrated pleasantly through her.

She pressed more tightly against his iron chest. "I've got the kitchen mostly cleaned up. The twins are off in a few minutes, so they won't be around to help with the mopping. I still have to do the deposit and deal with the twins' over-rings. That could take hours. Although sometimes I take that work home with me."

"Those are some pretty long hours you put in."

"The life of a businesswoman. When Paige hands over complete responsibilities, I don't want to think about how many more hours, but then…" She shrugged, not finishing. She'd almost said, "I don't mind because what else do I have?"

Tonight, things had changed. But her responsibilities had not. The phone at the front counter rang. "Oops, I need to get that."

Jake pressed a kiss to the crown of her head before she slid away from him. "Are those twins good babysitters?"

"They're very reliable, believe it or not, except with the cash register." Her grin sparkled and then she bounded down the aisle.

One of the twins looked up from refilling cola glasses with a big pitcher and laughed. "Hey, I heard that!"

Then Jake understood. This diner was important to Rachel because it was about her family. Family was everything to her. He respected that because it was important to him, too, and now he had one of his own. Across the table, Sally was drooping again. It was way past her bedtime. "Hey, princess. Are you done with that cocoa?"

She nodded, her eyes drifting closed again.

That was the final sign. She needed to be put to bed, and he'd have to wrench himself away from Rachel's presence. He didn't want to. It was a nice feeling, strange for a man who lived his rugged life, but not unwelcome. Funny how a few months ago he'd been happy with the challenge of being in the Middle East, with the missions he'd been assigned, and couldn't have imagined this. Being here, in this peaceful hometown diner with a kid needing to be tucked into bed. He would never have guessed he'd be wishing to hold sweet Rachel in his arms a little longer.

God sure moved in mysterious ways, but always for the best. Jake believed that. Rachel wanted her own family. Sally needed a new mother. And he needed… well, he didn't need anyone. It was hard to need anyone when he had a heart of iron.

The twin who'd laughed at Rachel's comment skidded to a halt at his table. "Oh, were you asking about tonight? I could watch her and stuff. You're just staying upstairs, right? You like Rachel, don't you?"

He could see Rachel out of his peripheral vision, chatting to someone on the phone, and the sight of her made the affection inside him flare dangerously. It was hard to admit, but he could understand the girl's question. Of course Rachel's family would be protective of her. "I like her very much."

"I thought so." Brianna—it said on her name badge—cracked her gum. "She's, like, the nicest person ever. You could marry her. Oh! Then she could move to Florida with you and, like, Ben lives there too, so she'd know people there. Rachel loves pale-pink roses. Just in case you want to give her some. Oh, want me to take Sally up for you?"

To be a teenager again and have that much energy. He fished the door key out of his pocket. "Her night-time storybook is on the nightstand by the bed. Sal, is it okay if you go with Brianna?"

But Sally was gazing up at the teenager in awe. She nodded and silently gave her hand when the twin reached for her.

"C'mon, sweetie. I'm a great reader. I do voices and everything. Okay?"

Sally clambered to her feet. She cast a worried look across the table.

"I won't be long, princess."

"'Kay." She trotted off alongside her newest heroine.

Rachel hung up the phone and knelt to say goodbye to Sally.

Bingo, he thought, watching how Rachel seemed to melt as she smoothed back the girl's stray curls with an affectionate hand. This path his life had taken was a good one, he decided. Rachel was the sort of woman a soldier like him needed, someone strong and independent, but so wonderful he couldn't wait to come home to her. Think of how great she'd be for Sally, and Sally for her.

Thank you, Father, he remembered to pray as Rachel released the girl, waved her through the door, and then disappeared into the office.

"Hey, I need to talk to you." Paige was no-nonsense as she slid into the booth across from him, her voice low but firm. "I know you're Ben's best friend and we are grateful for you hauling him to safety when he was shot, but you listen up. I don't want you using Rachel."

"That's not my intention, ma'am."

"What is your intention?"

"I'm going to marry her." He waited while Paige's eyes narrowed, as if she were trying to peer into him to see if he was worthy.

She frowned, as if she thought he came up short. "This isn't some kind of quick solution to your situation, with that little niece of yours, is it?"

"Still not convinced, huh?" Avoidance was better than admitting that on one level, Paige was right. But only because God had led him here and it was as if by heaven's grace that he realized how good Rachel could be for Sally.

And maybe Sally for Rachel. "Your sister would be a great wife. Why hasn't anyone swept her off her feet before this?"

"Rachel is shy and she's a homebody and a lot of men overlook her."

"Well, I'm not a lot of men."

"That remains to be seen." There was no mistaking the warning she sent him as she stood. "You'd better not hurt her."

"I would never hurt her."

Footsteps padded in their direction as a party of teenagers headed for the door. "Thanks, Miss McKaslin," one of them said. "The sundaes were real good."

"Good game, boys. See you next time." Paige

grabbed a tall blond boy from the crowd and gave him a squeeze. "I know, not in front of your friends, but I'm proud of you, running the winning touchdown. Are you going straight home?"

"Yes, Mom." He rolled his eyes, but he was clearly a good kid, and shook his head, apparently used to public humiliation as he wiggled away from her. "Bye."

"Boys." Paige glared right down at Jake. "I give the team free sundaes if they win, although it's probably a bad decision. Never give a male an inch, he'll take ten miles."

Someone has an attitude, Jake thought, as she marched away.

"Rache?" The remaining twin called out at the front door. "Do you want me to stay and mop?"

"No," came the answer from down the hallway. "Escape while you can."

"Bye!"

The last customers in the place, a clean-cut teenage boy and his girlfriend, crawled out from their booth, their voices low and tender as they ambled down the aisle hand-in-hand. Jake felt alone, not solitary as he always had, but lonely. See what caring for Rachel had done to him? He had to fight the urge to head into the kitchen just to see her. Just to be near her.

A bell rang at the front counter, calling Rachel from the back. "Are you ready to go?" she asked the young couple.

"Yes, and you promised to give me your hot chocolate recipe," the teenage girl answered.

"Jot down your e-mail address and I'll send it to you." Rachel gestured to the cup of pens on the counter as she took the order ticket and the boy's ten-dollar bill. The register chimed as she rang in the sale. "William, if you're still interested in the busboy job, give Paige a call sometime this weekend."

"Gee, thanks. I will." He took his change, grabbed a toothpick and held the door for his girlfriend.

Jake watched, not the boy, but Rachel. She gazed at the two with a wistful sigh. She was a romantic at heart, he realized. Pale-pink roses. Snowflakes and kisses. He knew next to nothing about romance, since his interests tended to be geared toward skydiving, motorcycle-riding and guns, but hey, he could figure it out as he went. He wanted to make her happy. He wanted to take care of her.

He didn't do true love, but he did responsibility just fine. And he cared deeply for her. How could anyone not?

"You're still here." She studied him over the top of the register while she pulled out the cash drawer. "It's going to be a long while until I'm done."

"You would be worth the wait."

His reward was her smile. She looked beautiful, fresh and bright in her simple worn jeans and a white long-sleeve T-shirt. There wasn't a thing fancy or sophisticated about her, not that he could see, and yet she rendered him speechless. "I have a slice of chocolate pie left in the case. Interested?"

"Tempted, yeah. But I'll pass. I don't think I've ever eaten this well."

"Then my work is done." Small dimples pinched into her cheeks, and his heart rolled over.

He hadn't lied to Paige. He cared for this woman more than was wise. He wanted to take care of her. He wanted to care for her. As she bounded away, he wanted to protect her from every heartache. Defend her from any trouble. Put more happiness into her life than she'd ever known before.

I've always wanted to have a good marriage and a happy family. Maybe because I lost my folks when I was young. He remembered what she'd said on their walk. He could give her what she wanted and more.

There was no time to waste. He slid out from the booth, bussed his cup and Sally's. He was ready to move this to the next level.

She had to be dreaming, that's what this was. A big wonderful dream where a fantastic man of integrity and honor was falling in love with her. Rachel squirted toilet cleaner around the bowl and beneath the rim. As she grabbed the toilet brush, she had to reconsider. She'd never been cleaning a bathroom in any of the dreams she'd had about the man she would marry. Which meant this night was real and no dream.

"I'm going to take this mess home with me so you don't have to deal with it." Paige poked her head in the ladies' restroom. "One day the twins are going to master the cash register. I suppose we have to be patient until then. If it doesn't drive us crazy first."

Rachel recognized the smile in her sister's voice. "I owe you big-time. I'd never get the deposit together. Those girls ran the till most of the night."

"I know. Are you going to be okay here alone? Should I take that man out with me when I go?"

"You don't like Jake?" Rachel knelt and gave the bowl a good scrub.

"I don't dislike him. Just thought I'd ask you what you wanted. I'm headed home, then. I've checked all the doors and windows. Everything's locked up. All you need to do is set the alarm."

"Thanks for your help tonight. Drive safely, okay? It's slick out there. Call me when you get home so I don't worry."

"That's my line, sweetie. I'll see you tomorrow early. Good night." The door swung closed, cutting out the tap of Paige's shoes on the tile.

Rachel gave the toilet a flush and scrubbed some more. As the water swirled, realization struck. She'd been so determined to keep from letting anyone know how much she liked Jake, and then so surprised that he felt the same way, she hadn't thought about the ramifications. Of course she knew Jake lived in Florida. He was stationed there. He was rarely stateside.

But she'd made a promise to Paige. What if this relationship progressed? He'd sounded as if he wanted it to, and heaven knew she was hoping. Then she would be forced to choose between a promise she'd made her sister and the encouragement she'd given to the man she was falling in love with.

Don't put the cart before the horse, she thought as she hauled the cleaner and brush to the next stall and gave the toilet a flush. We've had one date. Just one. And how on earth could they manage a relationship if he was stationed on secret bases throughout the Middle East?

Maybe she was getting her hopes up with this man for nothing. When she thought about it, there were too many obstacles. He had Sally as a priority. Then his duty. And she was stuck here in Montana, duty-bound to her family diner.

Disappointment trickled into her until she was cold. Until the happiness she'd felt after their kiss had completely faded. She scrubbed until the porcelain was clean and carried her cleaning supplies to the hall closet. She'd check on the dishwasher, see if a cycle was done before tackling the sinks and the counter. And then all that would be left was the floor.

Jake would be waiting, so she wanted to hurry, but her heart weighed her down. A true loving relationship took time and work and closeness, and even if he'd hinted he was interested in marriage, it was a long way from first date to wedding day. How could this ever work?

Maybe it was better to save her heart from falling any further while she still could.

The mop was gone from its hook in the closet. That was weird. Maybe it was in the kitchen and she hadn't noticed. Sometimes the evening cook gave the kitchen a swab when things were slow. Maybe he'd already cleaned up. Wouldn't that be nice? She grabbed her bottle of bleach mix and bopped down the short hallway to the kitchen. What she saw made her skid to a halt and blink. Was she dreaming again?

Jake was in the middle of the kitchen with his broad back to her, swabbing the mop across the floor. And not in a careless way either, but with sharp, effective strokes. He bent to douse the mop and wring the water from it and then went back to work, nudging the water bucket along with him with his foot, back and forth over and over, leaving spotless, gleaming tile in his wake.

He'd taken off his sweatshirt, and wore a long-sleeved navy T-shirt beneath, and she couldn't help noticing the way his hard muscles bunched and rippled beneath the knit fabric. In that moment, with only half the kitchen lights on, the partial shadows cast a powerful image of him, illuminating more than his physical self, but his essence as well. It was his spirit she saw, a core of honorable character, a warrior at heart, even here in a peaceful small-town diner in the middle of rural Montana.

He would never belong here, and she would never

ask him to give up who he was, who the Lord had made him to be.

He spoke without looking up from his work; he must have heard her footsteps. "Thought I'd pitch in. I've swabbed a few floors in my day, especially in boot camp."

She couldn't swallow past the lump of emotion wedged in her throat. "Pitch in, huh?"

"Yep. You may as well get used to it. I'm not a man to sit on my, uh, laurels." He grinned at her over his shoulder as he dunked the mop into the bucket and dowsed it. "I just want to help you."

"N-not many men wouldn't mind mopping a floor." She walked woodenly to the counter.

"I'm not just any man. I meant what I said tonight, Rachel. I don't waste my time, and I always know what I want. I'm here because I'd rather be cleaning your kitchen with you than anywhere else without you."

She set the bottle of cleaner down with a thunk. She couldn't believe him, could she? Men didn't just walk into a woman's life and change it, did they? Did he know what this meant to her? Maybe it was just a little mopping to him, but to her, it was so much more. She'd never known a man she'd dated to treat her like this. To pitch in, to help out or to say the things he did.

Her heart gave another tumble. It wasn't wise or prudent, no rational woman would let it happen, but this felt beyond her control. Love, sweet and true, rushed through her, filling her with brightness.

How strange. She'd always figured she would fall in love irrevocably and forever surrounded by roses and sunshine or on some momentous occasion, like Valentine's Day. She would have never thought love would happen to her like this, in a quiet calm glow, in the middle of the kitchen.

Emptiness echoed around her, or maybe it was the shadows, and the faint swish and clink of Jake's mopping in the dining room.

Maybe it *was* fitting, she realized, with the echoed memories of her life surrounding her. Her parents' happiness as they worked in this kitchen. Her childhood with her sisters and brother helping out or playing board games around the prep table. The ties of her family, of the past and the present both heartened her and tore at her.

The good experiences growing up in her family and in this diner had made her who she was. And the obligations that came from it felt smothering because she could not turn her back on this place or on her promise to Paige, just as she could not deny loving this man who pitched in to help her.

Torn, she went in search of clean rags, knowing this—as her life always was—in the Lord's care.

The snow fell like a blessing. Rachel brushed the softness from her cheek and turned the key in the dead bolt. The parking lot behind the diner was empty except for her trusty sedan and the twins' decades-old VW. "How do I properly thank you?"

"How about a kiss good-night?"

"That I can do."

It was a blessing to step into his arms. To have the privilege of his kiss. His lips brushed hers. The space between one breath and the next became infinity. She wrapped her arms around his neck and savored the secure feel of his arms wrapping around her.

What luxury, to be held by this wonderful man. She would not think about the future. She would not think at all. She wanted to savor the warm velvet of his kiss. The tender brush of his lips. The love like a light flaring to life within her in this one perfect moment.

He broke their kiss, and she could feel his love. He held her gently, and even in the half shadows of the night she could see the regret in his eyes. "I hate that I have so little time with you."

This is it, she thought. Where he says goodbye. Where he says it was nice, but he's moving on. And why wouldn't he say that, she reasoned as she laid her hand against his rugged jawline. They had entirely different lives, and very demanding and full lives. This love affair had to end. The pain of it gathered like a sharp blade at the base of her throat, slicing until she felt too raw to speak.

His fingers, so thick and powerful, caressed the curve of her face, making her heart ache. She pressed against his touch, and as he kissed her again, her heart opened. She couldn't deny that she loved him, and every time she was with him, she loved him a little more.

"It's not fair I have to leave." He pressed his forehead to hers. "Not when I've just found you. No woman has ever made me feel this way."

See, he was leaving. She knew he would be. There was no other choice for him to make. "I will never forget you."

"I'm going to make sure you won't." He brushed snowflakes from her face with her bare fingers.

She let her eyes drift shut at the rasp of his calloused fingertips against her skin. For all his strength, his touch was gentle. Did he know how much of her heart already belonged to him? She didn't think so, or why would he be talking like this? "Does that mean you want to stay in touch? Like friends?"

"No. I do not want to be friends with you."

"You don't?" The faintest hope fluttered in her soul.

"No. I want more." His head dipped to catch her lips with his. "I want everything."

"Everything?"

"I'm going to ask you to marry me."

"You are?"

"I've never met anyone like you, Rachel. And the way you make me feel—" Jake couldn't complete the sentence. He couldn't say the words that would render him vulnerable.

He could love her beyond logic and good sense, and trust her with everything he was, heart and soul. Which was why he had to hold on to his sense and his heart. Hiring a nanny for Sally would be easier. Finding a woman to marry who didn't affect him would be smarter. But the Lord had brought him here; He'd brought him to Rachel. Funny, beautiful, gentle Rachel.

He'd have to be strong and firm; he could do this for all their sakes. "You are perfect."

"Me? Oh, I don't think so. That just proves you don't know me. I lose my keys all the time, and I can't learn bookkeeping, and I have a thousand flaws. You have to have noticed that."

Her luscious hair was trying to escape the confines of her wool hat and silken strands were hanging out in random tangles. He smoothed the wisps and the act of touching her made the tenderness he felt for her flare like a launched missile. "You are perfect for me."

He watched her melt. She was amazing, this woman God had chosen for him and Sally. And the truth be told, even if heaven hadn't put him on this path to her, he would have fallen for her. He would have wanted her more than any woman in the entire world. "Here it is, almost midnight and snowing like we're in Alaska and I don't want to let you go."

"I know just how you feel."

"Then you don't mind if I spend as much time with you as I can while I'm here?"

"No. It would be a wish come true." Rachel bit her bottom lip, amazed at the honest words that just seemed to spill out of her.

She'd never felt this close to a man. She'd never had a man feel this way about her, and it was frightening and thrilling all at once. This was true love. "I'll see you in the morning. At Ben's sending-off party?"

His kiss was his answer, a gentle brush of lips, yes, but more. So much more. When his lips touched her, she felt the brush of his heart to hers. Of his soul moving with hers, and she held him tight, hope lifting her up. She would have floated home through the snowflakes dancing in the air except for Jake's rock-solid hands that held her firmly to the ground.

She'd been praying so long and earnestly for the right man; the very best man. She'd nearly given up hope. But some prayers were answered, and the answer was all the sweeter for the wait.

Chapter Twelve

"It's not the best weather for Ben and Cadence to start their move," Paige observed as she shouldered through the back door. "Now I wish they had left last night."

"The snow wasn't forecast." Rachel, who was waitressing this morning, slid a bottle of hot sauce into her apron pocket and grabbed two plates of giant cinnamon rolls from the warmer. "Now we're going to be worrying about them every moment from when they leave until they are safely through the entire state."

"I think the storm hit Wyoming, too. I heard it on the radio on the way in." Paige shrugged off her snow-dappled parka. "I dragged Alex here, not just for the party, but because we're short a bus person. If you see him lolling around, order him back to work. Got it?"

"Yes, ma'am." Rachel shouldered through the swinging door and into the dining room. The banners she and

Amy had come early to hang were glittering from the ceiling and stretched the width of the eating area. Good Luck! flapped overhead in black and gold as she hurried down the aisle.

Cousin Kelly looked up from her college textbook as Rachel eased the plate onto the table. "Are they here yet?"

"Ought to be any minute. I bet the roads are slow going. Would you like a refill?"

"Looks like that handsome dude of yours is here. When you get done seating him—" Kelly grinned "—then worry about my coffee cup."

Jake was here! Rachel whipped around and there he was, standing in the open door with snow tumbling in all around him. Sally clung to his side, and in his arms was a glass vase of pale-pink rosebuds. They were long-stemmed and gorgeous, and there had to be two dozen of the stunning flowers.

The sight of the roses wasn't what glued her feet to the floor. His gaze fastened on hers over the top of the delicate petals and she felt the brightness only he could bring to her soul. It was as if he saw the real Rachel McKaslin and beyond, deeper, to the dreams she held so close.

When he smiled, she fell in love a little more.

Vaguely she heard someone call, "They're here!" and the murmur of the customers, many of whom had come to send Ben and Cadence off, but it all seemed so far away.

Jake came to her, and she wondered if he felt this tug of awareness down deep within, and if he had the same sweet wish. *I'm going to ask you to marry me.* His words of last night lingered with her. *You are perfect for me.*

She'd come to fear she would never hear such beautiful and sincere words. And she stood in the diner she was duty-bound to take over and the conflict hit her like a blast of arctic wind. You would have been perfect for me, too. She laid her hand over her heart for the pain building there.

"Good morning, beautiful."

Longing filled her—chaste and sweet—as he came closer, and it was a longing that strengthened and expanded. She was blinded by joy as he set the exquisite flowers on the counter and leaned close. His mouth hovered over hers for a brief moment. She felt a click of connection as their hearts joined. Her soul stilled as he brushed his lips against hers in a brief, meaningful kiss.

"I had a hard time convincing a florist to open early, but Ben mentioned that Cadence had a friend who was a florist, so I did a little sweet-talking and you have two dozen roses. Do you like 'em?"

"I love them. They're gorgeous. And my very favorite. How did you know?"

"I'm good at reconnaissance."

"That's what I get for falling in love with a soldier."

The flowers were perfect and she was floating with happiness again.

"This is only the beginning of the good things I'm going to do for you." His hand cupped her jaw, loving and sure of his promise.

She was sure of his promise, too. He was a man who kept his word. She knew it; she could feel it in her heart, for it was inexplicably linked to his. Certainty filled her. This was the right man, sent from God above.

The bell above the door jangled cheerfully, and the sound cut into the bubble that seemed to have formed around them. The morning was the same as any other—the scent of fresh coffee, the sound of Paige's voice, and the chill of the winter wind slicing through the warm diner.

But it was no average, ordinary day. It felt like the first day of her life. It felt as though all the years up to this point had only been to bring her here, to this man who towered over her. His hand found her shoulder and rested there. Together they turned to face the door. The pleasant masculine scent of him, the shampoo in his hair and the detergent on his clothes made her dizzy, and she couldn't help letting her forehead lie against his chest.

With greater understanding, she watched her brother release the door he'd been holding for his new wife and lay his arm across her shoulder. The love between them was unmistakable as they exchanged intimate smiles, as if they knew what the other was thinking without the need for words.

The diner around them exploded with cheers. Family and friends packed the place, and congratulations and good luck wishes rang in the air, drowning out every other sound. Only then did Rachel realize she was still holding a plate with a cinnamon roll she'd promised the deputy. How could she move away from Jake?

"I'll take that." Paige whipped the plate out of her hand on her way by. She said nothing else, not even to send a look of disapproval Rachel's way.

But guilt stung, anyway. Rachel yanked herself away from Jake's wonderful chest, feeling cold and bereft as if she'd been shoved out in the snow. People were pushing by in the aisle wanting to greet the newlyweds and offer good-luck prayers for a safe journey. After slipping the cinnamon roll on Frank's table, Paige wrapped her arms around Cadence first and then Ben. Amy came rushing from the kitchen, where Heath had been helping with the extra cooking, and her diamond wedding set caught the light and shimmered as she joined in the hugging.

Everything is changing. Rachel didn't look back at Jake or the little girl clinging to his other side. She dutifully tugged the hot sauce bottle from her apron pocket and nudged it onto the edge of the deputy's table.

"For your eggs, Frank."

"First your sister and now your brother," Frank commented. "Looks like you might be next."

Heat flamed across her face. How did she answer that? Paige had overheard as she'd pulled back from the group. The hard set to her face said everything. Her older sister didn't look at her again as she hurried past, intent on seeing to something in the kitchen.

What am I going to do? Rachel felt as low as the snow melting on the rubber mat at her feet.

Ben's arms closed around her and his voice was a comfort as he spoke low in her ear, so only she could hear. "Jake's a decent guy. I trust my life to him every day. I think he's good enough for you, little sister."

Ben would understand. She swiped at the wetness on her cheeks. "What about Paige?"

"Have you talked with her about this?"

"No, you know how it is. I promised her. She stayed here all this time for us. And now with Alex graduating…" More people were pushing up to give their good-luck wishes and say their goodbyes. This was not the time. Rachel kissed her brother's cheek. "You two have a safe trip. Be so happy, okay?"

"I already am."

Bob Brisbane prodded in to shake hands with Ben, and as she sidestepped out of the way, someone grabbed her around the wrist and pulled. Amy hauled her close. "I was just telling Cadence all about you and Jake."

"What? First Ben and now you two. It's just—" She glanced over her shoulder where the flowers were being admired by her cousins Kelly and Michelle at the front counter. Jake and Sally had disappeared in the crowd, and she felt keenly alone without him near.

"Yep, it's what we thought." Amy sounded triumphant. "I've been praying for this, Rachel. For you to finally have the good man you deserve."

"He lives in Florida. He's away from home most of the year, just like Ben. And wait." She held up her hand, tucking away her pain because she didn't want Amy to know what this was costing her. "Before you go on about how Cadence is moving to Florida and how I could do the same, consider this. Jake and I are hardly even dating."

"Only a man who's serious brings you roses like that."

She blocked out Jake's words of last night. How he wasn't a man to waste his time. How he was serious about her, so serious he was looking into the future and seeing a marriage between them. "Florida is a long way away, and Jake and I haven't known each other that long. Love takes time."

"No," Cadence corrected gently. "Love takes heart."

"That's right." Amy's hold tightened as she tugged Rachel down the aisle in Jake's direction. "If this is something God means for you, then it will work out between Jake and you, and between Paige and you. It's in the Lord's hands, not yours."

"Right now, I'm in yours. You're taking me to him."

"Guilty, but then you know that about me. I want

what's best for my big sister. This is your chance, Rachel. Don't mess it up. Just believe." She gave her a small shove.

Rachel stumbled forward and there, around the corner where the window booths stopped and the table arrangements began, she saw him. Jake, who was coloring with a green crayon on the children's menu, right along with his niece. The sight of the strapping man next to the fragile little girl simply caught her heart all over again with love so pure she ached from its power.

"I'm going to work your shift today," Amy whispered. "And Heath and I will babysit tonight. Love, no matter what, is always a great blessing. Don't waste a minute of his time here."

Jake spotted her, put down his crayon and stood. He held out his hand for her to come join him. Everything faded, except for the love she felt for him. She floated forward to place her palm on his. They would have this day together. She couldn't wait to show him her world.

Rachel ignored the bite of frigid wind blowing hard against her face and driving the snow directly in her mouth as she tried to nudge Nugget out of the bitter wind. "Are you having fun yet?"

Jake was nothing more than a silhouette in the thick snowfall behind her, the image of western masculinity with his head bowed to the wind, his Stetson shielding his face from the precipitation, his broad shoulders set as he rode the equally impressive gelding he'd borrowed from Paige's son. "I don't call this fun."

"You're a city boy, that's why. Now, this is what I call living." She pulled her horse to a halt at the crest of the rise. The valley below spread out before them, misted by the thick veil of snow, and it was breathtaking and ethereal all at once. The gray light, the twilightlike shadows, the impressive rolling land so silent made the cold ride worth it. "This probably isn't exciting enough for you."

"You know the mountains behind us?"

"The Rockies?" The great mountains speared up and disappeared in the snow clouds, caught in a most severe part of the storm. "It wouldn't be safe to go up there right now."

"Well, give me an ice axe, crampons and a climbing buddy, and find me a glacier to climb. *Then* I'll be having fun." He halted Bandit and knocked the snow off his hat.

He could have been a hero in an old Western movie, and Rachel couldn't help a little sigh of appreciation. This man was hers. Somehow this would work out however the Lord saw fit, she would simply have to let go and let God handle it. Easy to say, not so easy to do. But up here, in the crisp, clean mountain air, she felt closer to the Lord and hoped understanding would come to her a little more easily, too.

"You can't get much ice-climbing at home in Florida."

"No, but there's sailing, jet skiing, waterskiing, diving, parasailing and hang gliding. That keeps me busy when I'm not training or on TDY."

"TDY. That means you're overseas, right?"

"Something like that. Temporary duty or tour of duty. Usually it means I'm in a chopper with mud on my face and a gun in my hand." He leaned close. "Have I told you how glad I am to be with you? I am, you know. I think this is the happiest I've ever been."

"Me, too." It was as if every shielded part of her opened, the places she kept safely hidden away. More vulnerable than she'd ever been with anyone ever, she dared to kiss him. And what a kiss it was. The moment his lips slanted over hers, more love for him lifted through her. She never knew that true love was like this, maturing more with every moment, every touch, every loving act. And this is only the beginning, she thought. *Please, Lord, I want to be with him so much.*

How she wanted to start each day with him. To come home to him after her work was done. To share the ordinary and average moments of grocery shopping and choosing a movie at the video store and paying bills and settling down to a quiet evening at his side. To have the right to kiss him like this, and more, for eternity.

When their kiss ended, neither pulled away. Their breaths rose in a single cloud as he kissed her forehead and her cheeks and the tip of her nose. How was it possible to love so much? She felt as if she'd come alive for the very first time—all over again.

"I've been afraid to ask when you have to go back."

"I have to report on Monday. They're going to keep me close to home for a little while until I get Sally settled. And then I'm back in the Middle East." He sidled his horse closer to hers and towered above her, blocking the wind and some of the cold. Leaning close to thumb the snowfall from her cheeks and eyelashes, he said, "There's nothing I can do about that. Orders are orders. You know that, because of your brother."

"Yep. We haven't seen him much at all since he graduated from PJ school."

"It takes more dedication to make a marriage work when a soldier is gone so much. My hat's off to him and Cadence. They seem to have a strong enough bond to make it."

"Of course they do. It's true love."

Jake's chest clutched. It was just what he thought. This peaches-and-cream, pale-pink-rose-loving lady was a pure romantic at heart. In the harsh realities he often faced as a warrior, he valued that about her. That she was as sweet and as good as could be.

Rachel's touch to his arm drew his attention. She pointed, and whispered. "A moose."

Sure enough like a ghost in the mist, a figure emerged, antlers held high. The animal's head was up and studying them with great suspicion. The musical tap, tap of snow was the only noise.

"Bullwinkle?" he whispered.

"No, I don't think so. He's not getting ready to come boss me into giving him some grain." She laughed, a quiet chime that sent the moose leaping into the underbrush. In the next instant the animal was gone, but it didn't feel as if they were alone.

Never more had Jake felt the steady calm of the Lord's presence, and he could feel the whisper in his heart. Ask her.

He'd planned on proposing after dinner on bended knee, with more roses he'd had delivered in collusion with Amy who'd agreed to have someone at the house to let in the florist. But with the fog of snow seeming to cocoon them from the strife and busyness of the world and the regal silence of the mountains surrounding them, he could think of no better place.

He dismounted and sank past his hiking boots into the snow. He ignored the sting of cold penetrating his jeans and wetting his socks.

"What are you doing? Don't tell me you're going to go find a glacier to climb."

"No, I'm going to do something much riskier."

"What on earth could that be?" Below the cuff of her knit cap, her jeweled eyes were sparkling as if he amused her greatly.

He held out his hand. "Come down and I'll show you."

"Okay." She easily swung down before him. "But you've gone completely pale. Are you all right?"

"No. Don't you know that a man always is pale when he's going down on one knee." He watched her eyes widen as he sank into the freezing snow, but his discomfort didn't matter. The surprise spreading across her lovely face did.

"What are you doing? I—" Her eyes widened and then she smiled all the way as if to her soul. *"Oh."*

"I need to ask you something."

Rachel shivered, but not from the cold. Could he tell she was trembling? That she was excited and scared all at once? The sight of the big man kneeling before her made her eyes blur. She couldn't believe it. And yet, when he took her hands in his, he was solid and real.

"Almost from the moment I saw you, I knew you were the one. The woman I would want to honor and cherish for the rest of my life. Will you marry me?"

Pure joy seeped into her soul, slow and steady, like a winter's sun rising.

"Marry you?" Her brain wasn't working, but her heart was. She tumbled to her knees and wrapped her arms around him, her cheek pressing against his wide chest. Snow flecked her face and caught on her lashes and she was laughing and crying all at once.

Jake was laughing, too. "Is that a yes? Or did I just make a huge fool of myself?"

"It's a yes. And you could never be a fool, not to me."

She met his kiss with one of her own. Held him tenderly as the snow fell like grace over them. Her eyes drifted shut and he tucked her against him, where she rested, despite the cold and the rising wind. Happiness warmed her as she held on tightly to this man who was her love, her heart and all of her future.

She was getting married!

I know you know what you're doing, Lord, but this marriage stuff is hard on a man. Behind the wheel of his rented SUV, Jake checked his watch, trying to act as if everything was fine. Beside him, Rachel was on her cell with Amy, asking how Sally was doing without her uncle.

"I've kept her so busy she's hardly noticed he's gone." Jake could hear Amy's cheerful answer in the quiet of the vehicle's compartment, but after a few more words, Rachel ended the call.

"You didn't tell her your news?"

"I wanted it to be our secret for a little while longer although I think she suspects." She blushed prettily. She was even more lovely when she was happy, for it radiated from her like light from the sun. As she slipped her hand on top of his, where it rested on the console, it struck him again how incredibly lucky he was.

His throat tightened. He'd been alone for so long, he'd never noticed how lonesome life was. In truth, maybe that's why he loved his work so much. It kept him from noticing what was missing. But not anymore. For better or worse, he was marrying Rachel, the sweetest, loveliest woman ever. She steadied him, and he felt as if he were making the smartest move of his life.

The traffic inched forward and he had enough room to turn into a plowed parking lot. Ice shone as he eased to a stop. "Looks like we're here. Are you ready for this?"

She didn't answer. She was staring at the jewelry store's elegant lit sign. "I—uh." She flushed again. "I didn't expect this."

"I wanted you to pick out the ring you want. Any one you want." He turned off the engine and pulled the emergency brake. "Are you ready?"

She sparkled with a quiet joy and made him feel ten feet tall. He wanted nothing more than to make her happy as much as he could. Any way he could. When he helped her from the vehicle, he'd never felt so important. The way she looked at him with such pure affection weakened the titanium shield he'd secured around his heart.

"Hello Mr. Hathaway?" A pleasant woman in a business suit met them at the door. "I'm Carol. We spoke on the phone. And you must be Rachel. Congratulations on your engagement. Please, come with me. I have a room all ready for you, along with quite a selection of our loveliest diamonds."

Even hours later, after an incredible dinner at the

area's finest restaurant, he could not forget how great it felt to know he was giving Rachel her dream. He'd sat at her side and offered his opinion on the array of fine rings he'd asked the store to set out for her. His bride-to-be was far more elegant and classy than any of the exquisite stones. When he slipped the diamond she finally chose on her finger, he could not hold back the adoration for her beating in his heart.

Chapter Thirteen

What a beautiful night. It seemed to be a promise from above, Rachel thought, as the last snowflakes danced lazily against the windshield. The defroster was on high to drive away the gathering chill of the night that penetrated the passenger compartment. It looked like it was going to be an early and long Montana winter. But would she be here to see it?

She gazed down at her left hand and the marquis-cut diamond set between two smaller stones gleamed in the glow from the dash lights. The ring, as beautiful as it was, felt foreign on her finger.

She still couldn't believe it. She was getting married to Jake. As he shifted into four-wheel drive for the last stretch of driveway, she realized this was where they'd first met. She tried to imagine what he'd thought of a woman racing down the road waving a broom and wearing her big fluffy slippers.

Who would have thought that evening, when she'd been so exhausted and not expecting her one perfect man, that her life would change the very moment they met?

Jake pulled into the carport, where drifted snow pulled at the tires and they skidded to a slow sideways stop. "How's that ring feel?"

"Perfect because it's from you."

"It's your hand that looks so beautiful." He leaned across the gearshift to kiss her, this woman who tied him up in so many confusing knots. When her lips met his, those knots pulled a little tighter. What he felt for her was a powerful thing. How was he going to keep it under control? When he pulled away, he didn't miss the dreamy cast to her face. Moonlight filtered through the icy window to burnish her with a rare, platinum light. He felt too much.

He welcomed the bite of the frigid temperatures that assaulted him the instant he stepped foot into the night. He helped Rachel from the vehicle with care. She might be a capable woman, but she was also going to be his wife. He remembered the way his dad had always held the doors for Mom. They had been happy together. His father's words of advice back then meant little, but came back as great wisdom now. *Treat her right, son. You aren't here for yourself, but for her.*

Good advice. Because of Rachel, he'd be able to get back to work. Sally would have a kind woman to raise her. And in return, he was giving her what mattered most. A marriage. A family. His respect and his honor.

That was a good marriage in his book. And he thanked the Lord for this fine woman. Maybe he wasn't thankful for the knots in his guts, but he could survive the discomfort. For Rachel, he felt ready to do anything.

"I need to talk to Paige first thing in the morning." She leaned into him.

He put his arm around her and drew her close, protecting her from the wind and making sure she didn't slip on the ice. It was his job now to care for her, and it meant a lot to him. Filled him with a purpose he'd never known. "Is there anything I can do to help you?"

"No, thank you." She snuggled against him a little closer. "This is something between Paige and me. All I can do is explain what's happened and see what comes from it. Thank you, though. It's nice to know that you're here for me."

"Baby, that's something I plan on being as much as I can. We're a team now. I care about what matters to you."

"No wonder I love you so much." On the top step, she went up on tiptoe to kiss his cheek, the sweetest gesture.

His chest filled with a welcome sense of wonder. It was going to be really nice to belong with her.

She unlocked the front door and disappeared into the unlit foyer. He stomped the snow from his boots before following her, and he sensed something was wrong. Someone was in the house. He could smell a faint perfume, and there was that awareness that made his neck prickle. Someone was watching him in the dark—

"Surprise!" The lights flashed on at the same moment he saw shadows move in the darkened archway.

Years of training had already kicked in and he was standing in front of Rachel, between her and the danger which was her family rushing toward her with arms outstretched.

"Did he propose?" one of her cousins asked.

"Let's see the ring!" Amy demanded.

As the women gathered close around Rachel to ooh and aah, Jake wished he could shrug off the charge of adrenaline pumping through him as easily as he slipped out of his coat. He caught Paige's hard, measuring gaze and didn't fault her for it. She'd been in charge of the family and watching over Rachel for a long while.

He had the gist of what that would be like, because the thought of watching over Rachel battered at his defensive shields. He couldn't deny she made him feel a mess of weak and vulnerable things that couldn't be good for a man—things that were never wise for a soldier. He'd seen too much war, too many wounded, too much heartbreak, and the only way he could deal was to keep those shields up. It was all he knew to do.

"Uncle Jake?" Sally wandered down the hallway, scrubbing her eyes. She was still dressed, but she'd obviously fallen asleep in one of the bedrooms. Maybe

Amy had carried her back there. Unmistakable relief flashed across her pixie face and she flung her arms wide.

He went down on both knees to draw this dear child against him where he hoped she felt secure as her arms wrapped right around his neck. "I didn't mean to be gone so long, cutie pie. Rachel and I just went out to a nice dinner, but we're back now."

Instead of comforting her, his words seemed to make everything worse. Her little body drew as tight as a tensed bowstring and her arms squeezed him until she cut off his air supply. So he rose, cradling her weight against him, murmuring low as he carried her back down the hall.

A faint golden glow led him through the shadows where it became a night-light in the shape of a crescent moon and five-pointed star next to a canopy bed. Gauzy pink drifted from the frame overhead, matching the flowers on the bedspread. Rachel's room, of course. A knit blanket was rumpled, as if tossed aside.

He sat on the edge of the comfortable mattress, holding his niece in his arms. He might be helpless to stop the pain that had a hold on her heart, but the solution to her problem was in sight. It was only a matter of a wedding. "I've left you longer than this before. Why the tears, sweet girl?"

She sniffled against his shirt. "Cuz I don't wanna go back."

"Go back where?"

"To Mrs. Thompson's. Sh-she was n-nice, but I wanna stay w-with you." She sobbed and burrowed into his shoulder.

"Who said anything about you going back into foster care? I told you, we're together now. I promised you, didn't I? No one's going to take you away from me. You come live with me. It's a done deal. You can't change your mind now."

"I c-can c-come with you and R-Rachel?" A sob shook her little body.

So that was it. The lightbulb went on in his head. Of course, why hadn't he realized she would have worries of being left alone at this important change in his life? He pressed a fatherly kiss to her brow, because that's what he was, not just an uncle, but her father figure too. "That's why I'm marrying her. For you, princess."

"Oh." She gave a last sniff and smiled through her tears. "Okay."

At that moment, Rachel padded through the door, her face shrouded in the room's shadows. With the light to his back, he couldn't see the expression on her face, but she froze, her slender form tensed.

Then he realized what he'd said. And how that might have sounded, as if the only reason he'd proposed was for Sally. While that was true, it wasn't the whole truth. Not judging by the sinking feeling in his chest and the gathering fear like clouds before an impending tornado. Had she overheard him? Did she think he didn't want her? He'd give his life before he'd want to hurt her in any way. It was as if his blood stalled in his veins and his lungs had forgotten how to draw in air while he waited for her reaction. While he dreaded her reaction.

"Oh, Jake." Her voice sounded hollow.

He braced himself for the worst. Groped for the right words to try to fix this. *Please, Lord, let me be able to make this right.*

Then she kept talking. "I never thought this might be too much for Sally. Sweetie, do you want me to make you some cocoa?"

He couldn't believe it. Relief left him dazed. *Thank you, Lord.* How could he not adore this woman who tried to make every hurt better with hot chocolate? Sally nodded against his chest, but she still didn't look at Rachel. He held her tight. He had to wrestle down the weak emotions threatening to overtake him.

"I'm so sorry, Jake. I guess my sister figured out what we were up to." Rachel's ring shimmered in the shadows as her hands flew to cover her heart. "I didn't want Sally to find out this way. My sisters meant well with this little get-together."

"I know." He studied the ring on her finger. His ring. "I want to marry you now. I don't want to leave for Florida without you."

"You're leaving tomorrow."

He swallowed. "I know. I have to report Monday morning, but after that I'll know my schedule. I'll be training some of the new students while I'm stateside. I'm putting in a request to stay at least through the end of the year. If we get married right away, we'll have most of December together before I go away for, well, probably six to nine."

Six to nine months. So much for the dream of marriage. She was jumping into the reality with both feet. "I won't have time to plan much of a wedding. I'd always wanted—" She stopped the image forming in her mind, the one she'd envisioned more times than it was possible to count. The picture of the town church, where her parents were married and she was baptized, soft with candlelight and scented with roses.

Her sisters and cousins would be draped in pale-pink bridesmaid's dresses and lined up at her side, and her family and friends would be gathered as witnesses. Pastor Bill would be standing before her, and she would be wearing her mother's wedding dress.

But everything she'd ever wanted for her wedding was not as important as the man who would be at her side. It wasn't the wedding but the vows, not the setting but the marriage that mattered.

"What's best for you?" she asked. Those dreams of a wedding began to float away, but she didn't mind, for the greatest dream of all was right in front of her. "Would it be better for you if I came down to Florida to get married? Don't get me wrong, I would love to have you come here, but we could have more time together."

"You choose. You tell me when and I'll show up to marry you."

"That's a promise?"

Was that a note of worry he heard? Jake wondered. Somehow it made it easier to open up a little. To see that they both had so much riding on this. So much to lose. He fought down the wave of emotion trying to hook him like a riptide. "Not only is it a promise, but I'll give you my credit card. Plan a wedding for here, or fly down there and we'll have a quick ceremony. You decide. I just want you to be happy. From here on out, that's what I live to do."

"That's what I plan to do, too. To make you and Sally so happy. I—" She swiped at her eyes before her emotions gave her away. She was so in love with this man. More than she'd ever thought anyone could be. The thought of spending the rest of her days with him filled her with such gratitude. How could she ever ask for more?

"Come here, gorgeous." Jake held out his hand and pulled her close. Sally yawned against his chest, her eyes barely open.

Everything seemed to click into place. Tomorrow, she would have to say goodbye to these two people who were now the most important people in her life. She would start packing up her life, talk Amy into taking this house, and book a ticket to Florida. She was ready for this beautiful new start the Lord had given her.

As if Jake felt the same way, he leaned to press a kiss to her cheek. Sweet as could be, infinitely tender, there was no mistaking the love between them. And a great love it would be, she vowed. She couldn't wait to stand before God and say the blessed vows that would make her Jake's wife.

It was decided. "Then we're going to have a Florida wedding. Sally, are you going to be my maid of honor?"

"With flowers 'n stuff?" The little girl perked up, rubbing her still-wet eyes.

"Any kind of flowers you want. Is that a deal?"

Sally nodded, her curls bobbing.

I want to hug you, little girl, until all your hurt is gone. Rachel knew it wasn't her right yet, but she laid a hand on the child's tiny shoulder, so fragile to the touch, and willed all the comfort she could from her heart to Sally's.

"Thanks, Rachel." Jake's baritone warmed when he said her name. As if he loved her as greatly as she loved him.

The Lord had given her a great blessing, two for the price of one. A sacred gift she would cherish for all the days of her life. She would never be able to thank God enough for these two people or this beautiful day. A bright, loving future stretched out before her, one spent taking care of them, and maybe a baby or two to come. Joy bloomed through her as she promised to be back with two cups of cocoa. She couldn't help glancing back as Jake settled onto the bed and reached for a child's book left on the nightstand.

Now, to face Paige. This wasn't the way she wanted Paige to find out about this either. She owed her older sister so much. If Paige wasn't happy, then Rachel didn't know what she would do. How could she turn her back on her sister? How could she give up this bright new future?

Paige was in the kitchen at the stove, stirring the contents of a saucepan. So tall and lovely and looking so like their mother, Rachel did a double-take. The past felt close enough to touch on this night when she could see her future so clearly. *Help me to say the right things, Lord. Never would I want to hurt my sister.*

But Paige was as happy-looking as she'd been earlier when Rachel had walked through the door with Jake. "I should leave, so you and Jake can have some time alone, but I have something to say to you. I don't think it can wait."

"This just happened so fast, Paige. I didn't mean for it to be like this. I wanted to talk to you first, because if you aren't okay with this—"

"—I've been giving it a lot of thought—"

"—then you need to tell me the truth. Because I can't leave here if it's not all right—"

"It's all right." Paige wrapped her in a brief hug. "No one expected this to happen. You and Jake fell in love. This is your turn to live your dream, Rachel. To really grab hold of what matters in life. So don't waste this chance. Forget about the diner."

"But what about your plans?"

"I'll figure something out. Maybe one of the cousins would be interested in taking over. Do you want some hot chocolate?" Paige returned to the saucepan to give it a few more stirs.

Mom's secret cocoa recipe was the cure for all heartaches, and the memory of being young in this kitchen with Mom at the stove and warming chocolate scenting the air made her throat burn with tears. "I always thought I'd be raising my own kids in this house."

"Jake lives in Florida. Sounds like you'll be raising them there."

"Yeah." The thought made her sad and blissful at the same moment. How could so many polar emotions be inside her at once? "I'm really leaving."

"Don't say that out loud because you're breaking my heart." Paige kept her back firmly turned as she reached down a set of mugs. Her voice sounded thick with unshed tears. "If that man doesn't make you happy, all you have to do is tell me and I'll put some sense into him. Okay?"

"Okay." Rachel grabbed the marshmallow fluff from the refrigerator door and twisted off the lid. "You can stop being my big sister now."

"I'm never going to stop being that. What are we going to do without you?"

Rachel couldn't speak. She spooned fluff onto the cups of steaming cocoa that Paige poured. Amy had taken off for the West Coast instead of graduating from high school and had been gone for several years. Ben had joined the air force, never to return for more than a brief stay. And although Rachel had gone to college, she'd come back.

But not Paige. She'd stayed to do the tough work of holding the family together, making a small-town diner do a good enough business to support all of them, all while raising her own wonderful son. "I'm going to be gone for a long time."

"This is just occurring to you?"

She nodded. "The reality is starting to sink in. I'm getting married. Finally. He's such a wonderful man. I know he'll be good to me."

"Of course he will be." Amy burst into the room. "Or we'll kick some sense into him. I don't want you to leave, Rache. What are we gonna do without you?"

"I—I don't know what I'm going to do without both of you. This is supposed to be happy, getting engaged. I always thought of getting married as adding to my life. Not changing it."

"Marriage is like nothing else. It changes everything." Amy grabbed the chocolate syrup from the fridge and popped the cap. She joined Paige, who'd returned to the counter. "Then again, marriage is one of God's great blessings."

"Well, so are sisters." Paige's eyes were filling with tears, but she was always so strong, Rachel had never actually seen a single tear fall. Never. "Here. Take these to that man of yours and that sweet little girl. You belong with them now, but know this. Your home will always be here, too."

Love and hot chocolate, the family cure-all. Rachel couldn't speak as she took the cups in her hands, trying hard not to spill them. This is a beginning, not an end, she told herself firmly as she disappeared down the dark hall. Everything she knew and loved was here.

No, not everything. She paused in the doorway, mesmerized by the low murmur of Jake's voice. How was it she could love this man even more than her life? He was her family now, and little Sally her daughter. Already she had them to love. And it made the pain of knowing she would leave this place vanish. Her own husband and a child to care for.

Contentment spread through her, sweet like the warm rich cocoa she carried until nothing remained but gratitude. Jake grinned at her over the top of the book he was reading out loud. Her soul sighed, and she was fulfilled.

She was truly loved, at long last.

Chapter Fourteen

Florida was hot, even in the winter. Rachel squinted into the foggy mirror in the hallway off the base's chapel, afraid sweat was beading on her forehead and her veil would be in danger of becoming plastered to her face.

She so wanted this short ceremony to be perfect, although nothing so far had gone to plan and she felt weary from struggling to right it. The last week she'd spent in Montana, after Jake and Sally had left, had been a whirlwind of packing and making arrangements and saying goodbyes. She'd given up her whole life to be here with Jake.

If Jake hadn't sent her roses every day they were apart, she wouldn't have made it this far, because the obstacles had continued to mount. Her plane had been diverted due to a thunderstorm and she'd spent hours circling over Tampa, gazing down at the incredible scenery and feeling so out of place. She'd left four feet of snow behind and near-blizzard conditions that had almost kept the plane from taking off in the first place.

Add lost luggage, traffic jams, Jake being called at the last minute into the field for training and she'd seen him only at the courthouse to get the marriage license.

"Don't worry, you look lovely." Cadence, who had stepped in as a true sister over the last few tough days, smoothed the back of the veil. "Jake is going to take one look at you and he won't believe how lucky he is."

"I'm the lucky one." The Lord knew it was true. She pinned on her mother's cameo, the one Paige had given her as a goodbye gift. Once the delicate clasp was secure, she took a steadying breath.

Jake was waiting to marry her. This moment was everything she'd ever wanted and prayed for. It seemed as if heaven were smiling, or maybe that was just the joy bubbling within her soul, as she took her first step on the plain brown carpet that would lead her down the aisle and to her groom, to the man God had found for her.

The ivory silk of her mother's wedding gown whirled and whispered as she took another step following Cadence. Jake was there, looking like a promise made and kept in his dress blues. He stood solemnly before the simple altar with Sally leaning against his side, her eyes wide with uncertainty. All eyes turned to Rachel, but it was Jake she saw. Jake she *felt* deep in her soul.

I never realized how deeply sacred a wedding was. As she stood there, poised at the aisle where simple wooden pews marched the length of the small chamber, Rachel felt it. More than the dreams of a little girl wondering and wishing for this day. More than the committed, emotional ties of a woman to her man. It was as if heaven waited, too, watching to celebrate the blessed gift of true love, a victory in a wide world that included heartache and cruelty.

The opening notes of the bridal march filled the chapel as sweetly as grace.

Ben offered his arm. "Are you ready for this, little sister?"

"Without a doubt." She slipped her arm in his and they moved forward together. Every step brought her closer to Jake. She was not nervous. She was certain.

As the minister asked, "Who gives this woman?" and Ben answered, "I do," she accepted her brother's kiss on her cheek and his good wishes, knowing she would not need them. The blessing of Jake's love was enough. Their love would be strong enough. Jake held out his hand, and there was no need for words. She knew he felt the same.

"Dearly beloved," the minister began those time-honored words, the ones she knew by heart. The words she'd been waiting to hear like this, at Jake's side.

Then the sound of the minister's voice faded away and it was like being underwater in a warm and clear ocean. There were the two of them—her and Jake—his hand steady and sure, and his gaze fastened on hers. It was as if an unseen current flowed between them, beyond the physical, to their spirits within.

She realized true love was greater than two people. More powerful than both man and wife combined. It was a force that also connected them to a greater love, a greater purpose. And she felt awed by the calm that filled her. She repeated those sacred vows to love and honor and cherish.

The surge of love that overtook her was unconditional and infinite and there was nothing that would ever diminish it. Not sickness. Not hardship. Not even death.

As Jake slipped the ring on her finger, a diamond band to match the solitaire, she saw the emotion gathering in his dark eyes. He might stand warrior-tough, but he had a good loving heart. There was no mistake about that. When he lifted her veil and his kiss sealed their vows, happiness like no other filled her. Now they were two hearts and one soul.

It was surreal carrying Rachel through the doorway of his modest town house. After a celebration supper with Ben and Cadence and Sally at a fancy seafood restaurant not far off base, he left Sal with his good friends, promising to pick her up bright and early in the morning. Here he was, carrying a silk-clad bride into his very beige living room.

No visions of grandeur and luxury, just a comfortable couch he'd bought secondhand from a squad member who'd gotten out, and battered-looking end tables. He hadn't realized just how shabby his things were.

Please don't be disappointed, he thought. She'd spent last night with Ben and Cadence to save the cost of a hotel room, and training had run late, so there had been no time to show her what she was getting into.

"Oh. You have a view." Her eyes were shining. "And there's the beach. I could get used to this."

"Yeah?" That was good, because he'd be stuck in Florida for some time to come. "I've got three more years left. I know this isn't what you're used to, but I sure hope I can make you happy here."

"I'll be happy anywhere as long as I'm with you. You are my everything now." She blushed rosily and she'd never looked more amazing. This woman was his wife now, this incredible lady, and he couldn't stop the rush of affection that would take him over if he let it.

It's gratitude, he told himself as he set her on her slippered feet, not love. He was deeply grateful for a woman he respected and who was so kind. She was exactly the kind of lady he'd hoped to find some day.

The Lord sure worked in awesome ways, he thought, as he nudged the door shut with his foot. Awesome because He'd brought the exact right wife into his life when he was at a loss as to what to do with Sally. The timing was God's he knew. Sally wasn't the only reason Rachel was wearing his wedding ring. No, he'd been at a loss for a long time, he could see that now that she was standing in his living room.

This house he lived in was suddenly a home. The life he'd filled only with the challenge of work now had a deeper purpose: to take care of Rachel with all of his might. He never wanted to fail this woman entrusted to him.

"How about a walk on the beach?" he suggested, smoothing back the thick bounce of curls that had tumbled against her face.

She pressed against his hand, her eyes drifting shut, as if valuing his touch.

"I would love to. But I've got to change. I'm not sure how easy it would be to walk in the surf like this." She gave her skirt a twirl and the full hem flared out to reveal her white ballet slippers. "Where are my things?"

"Ben brought them over this morning. I put them in the main bedroom. Up the stairs. It's the first door on your left."

"Okay. I'll be right back. I'm psyched. Wow! We live on the beach." They were a team now, and she was a wife!

Her life kept getting better and better, Rachel thought as she blew her husband a kiss, gathered up her skirt and dashed up the stairs. The gentler light of early evening was thinning, and she so wanted to have the daylight left to go on a long walk with her husband. They would be just another married couple, out for an evening stroll, hands linked, hearts content.

She half expected Jake to be coming up behind her, so she left the door ajar, spotted her suitcase under the wide picture window that gazed through the spears of palm leaves at the endless stretch of turquoise water. Pale sunshine poured through the slatted blinds and she turned the wand to close it. The light dimmed, and she gazed around the room she would be sharing with Jake.

The bed looked wide enough to be a queen-size. It was neatly made with a pale-blue bedspread covering it, and four plumped pillows in matching blue shams. Two mismatched nightstands sat at either side of the bed, holding matching lamps and a phone, an alarm clock and a thick, tattered military suspense paperback were crowded on the nightstand to the right side. That must be where Jake slept. And that meant she would be on the left side.

It gave her an odd, thrilling joy to think about the night to come. What a blessing to be held and loved by her husband, she thought, and, feeling bashful, decided not to think anymore about it.

The phone rang, echoing in the quiet house, then died in mid ring. Jake must have grabbed it downstairs. She waited. Sure enough she could hear the mumble of his voice. Maybe it was Sally calling. She hadn't been sure about staying with Cadence, who'd been spending a lot of time watching her over the past few weeks. As Cadence had said, now Sally was her niece to watch over and spoil as much as possible.

I hope Sally's not having a hard time away from Jake, Rachel thought as she managed to loosen the hooks-and-eyes at the back of her dress. The poor girl had been through enough. If she was afraid, then they would swing by and take her on their evening walk, too.

She knelt and popped open her largest suitcase. In a half a second she'd grabbed her favorite pair of walking shorts and a light T-shirt and headed for the attached bathroom. She wasn't surprised by how clean and tidy everything was. Jake had clearly picked up and cleaned to make a good impression for her.

The small room had a high window that let in light as she pulled her hair into a ponytail and changed into her comfy clothes. Carefully, she gathered up the treasured dress and laid it out on the bed. No sign of Jake, so he must still be on the phone. She slipped her feet into her old sneakers and trotted down the steps.

He *was* on the phone, talking earnestly and low to whoever was on the other end of the line. He looked serious so maybe it was military stuff. She wandered into the kitchen and admired the cozy room. The appliances were a good decade old, but in good repair and very handy. She could imagine whipping up dinner while she waited for bread dough to rise and talking to Jake over the breakfast bar all the while.

Could anything be more perfect? This cute little duplex, full of good views and cozy places and a husband and child to care for. This was her home. This was her life. She was infinitely grateful.

She spotted a small bottle of water on the top shelf of the fridge and not much else, and thought how exciting this would be. To discover new favorite spots like grocery stores and coffee places and used bookstores. Things she could do with Jake and Sally. What an adventure it would be.

Brimming with happiness, she let herself outside, leaving Jake to finish his call in privacy. She sat down on the concrete top step and let the breeze off the ocean brush against her face. It was like a whole new world the Lord had given her, full of promise and good things. She could *feel* it. She thought of Paige and Amy, who would be handling the Friday-night supper rush about now. Tonight was the last high-school football game of the season and more snow had been expected, she knew. And she was staring at the Gulf of Mexico, wearing shorts!

The door behind her rasped open and Jake bounded down next to her, all business and tight energy. One look at his hard face told her something was wrong.

"Is it Sally?" Her heart jumped. "Is she okay? She was so quiet today, she's not sick—"

"No. I've got field training tonight. It's a drill. There's not a single thing I can do about it. I've tried to get out, but I can't. You get the call, and you go. It's a mock emergency scenario and I've got to grab my gear and get rolling."

Rachel studied the naked apology so stark on his handsome features and she knew with a sinking feeling that she had to let him go. It was as if the sun dimmed. "This definitely makes me feel like a military wife. You're sure you have to go, huh? No, don't answer that. I know you do. I just don't want you to go."

"Neither do I. Baby, I'll make it up to you. I swear. I've got to run."

"I know." She trusted him, she knew he would make sure they'd have another evening that would be special together. Although this, their first night as husband and wife was not what she'd expected. She tapped down the rising disappointment.

"Thanks, baby. I'll be back." He kissed her quickly and bolted away. The door clicked shut. Less than a minute later she heard a pickup roar to life. His red truck sped down the driveway between the units, honked and disappeared around the corner.

Now what? Rachel still couldn't believe she was sitting alone on her wedding night. The sun sank lower, casting a rosy glow directly into her eyes. She squinted and tried to remember where she'd put her sunglasses. The phone rang inside. Maybe that was Jake. Maybe his field emergency thing was cancelled. A girl could hope!

She snatched it up on the third ring. "Hello?"

"Rachel." Cadence sounded unruffled, and Rachel

remembered that Ben was on Jake's team. Maybe he would have gotten the same call. "I bet you've suddenly found yourself without plans for the evening. How about coming over and watching a movie with Sally and me? We've got some good family favorites to pick from."

"I'll be over." See, God never closed a door without opening a window. She'd spend the evening with her new niece and her sister-in-law. And maybe Jake would be back before bedtime. She left a note, just in case.

Jake sat in the belly of the chopper with his pockets heavy with extra ammo and protectively holding his M-4. He couldn't get Rachel out of his thoughts. Not good for a soldier when lives depended on his absolute mastery of his emotions and iron self-control.

He'd had to leave her on their wedding night. That couldn't be a good sign. Not at all. What if she doubted his commitment? The knots in his chest that thinking of her always brought him stretched so tight, he couldn't breathe.

What defense did a man have against the power a woman could have on him, and against the strength of love that he could feel for her?

"Hathaway. Focus, man."

He looked up to see his squad leader snapping his fingers at him.

Not good. They were at the mock LZ, and his team

members were standing, preparing to fast-rope down under simulated hostile fire. He brought his mind to the task ahead, but his heart was heavy. Something was going to go wrong, he could feel it. Very wrong.

With Sally's cold hand tucked safely in hers, Rachel held the screen door and helped the girl find her way into the dark house. She hadn't thought to leave a light on, mostly because she'd been so disappointed she hadn't thought too far ahead. She fumbled along the wall for a light switch and didn't find one.

Sally let go in a hurry and her footsteps sounded impatient as she crossed the living room. Faint shadows crept between the blinds to give the furniture shape, enough to navigate around. There was a click and a lamp turned on, illuminating the wariness on Sally's usually cute face. Rachel had the feeling Sally wasn't going to be cute tonight.

She's lost a mother and had to move away from everything she knew, Rachel reminded herself. Her heart softened for this child who was hers now to nurture. She trusted the Lord to guide her through this, because she was going to need some big-time help. Jake getting married must be a scary change for a little girl who'd already lost her stability. It made sense she would be worried. "Tell you what, you run up and change into your jammies and I'll whip up some cocoa and be up to read to you."

"It's too hot for cocoa."

"Okay, how about some chocolate milk? I noticed a carton in the fridge. I'll—"

"No." Sally glared at her and crossed her hands over her chest, as if preparing for a fight. "I want Uncle Jake to get it for me."

Uh-oh, this is going to be harder than I thought. Rachel headed to the kitchen anyway. "I'm going to make some for myself."

Sally's answer was to storm upstairs. Rachel found two blue glasses in a pretty bare cupboard, wondering how to help Sally the most. She was afraid, and Rachel knew something about that. Me, too, kiddo. Love was an act of faith, that was for sure. She poured a cup of milk and sipped it. The comforting chocolate and blessed cold did wonders for her. It was still warm at nine-thirty at night. Florida weather was nice, but it would take some getting used to.

The empty kitchen echoed around her with promises of tomorrow. Things would be better in the morning. Jake would be back, she felt sure, and she'd be frying up breakfast. If there was food to prepare.

A quick inventory of the pantry told her there was a half-used bag of pancake mix, and the prerequisite syrup and jam to go with it. She found half a carton of eggs in the door of the fridge and a half-pound of bacon in the freezer. She set that on a refrigerator shelf to thaw and, satisfied, locked up, turned off the lights and snatched Sally's overnight bag on the way to the stairs.

No light shone down the short and narrow hallway. She knocked on the first door on her right—no answer. "Sally?" She cracked the door a little and saw the faint dusting of moonlight sifting through half-slatted blinds.

The silver glow fell on a mattress on the floor, made up with fresh sheets and a blanket and a plump pillow. A man's clothes hung in the open closet and fatigues were neatly folded on the floor. Jake's things? No, that didn't make any sense. Maybe the mattress was for guests. It would be handy if one of her sisters could come down to stay. And those were extra clothes of Jake's. That's all.

"Sally?" She went in search of the girl's room and stopped outside the next room. A faint glow that crept beneath the door told her a television was on. She knocked and turned the knob. "Sally? I've brought your bag."

The only answer was friendly electronic music beeping and bopping from the TV. Rachel pushed the door open enough to see a child's video game flashing on the screen. Sally sat crossed-legged on her bed, still in her cute turquoise shorts set, not at all ready for bed. And with the way she stared intently at her game, working the controls with concentration, she wasn't interested in bedtime just yet.

Okay, she's testing me. This was normal, typical kid

behavior. After all, the two of them didn't really know one another. Sally didn't know that it was okay to trust her, and that already Rachel loved her so much. With patience, she'd figure it out. "Bedtime. Let's get out your pajamas."

"I'm not tired." Sally didn't move her eyes from the screen. She spoke more like a robot than the sweet kid she was in Jake's care.

Rachel unzipped the bag and tossed the pink jammies onto the bed. "Suit up, and we'll settle down to read."

"No." Sally gave the pretty garments a shove off the bed and then went right back to her game. "I don't have to do what you say. You're not my mom. You're not even my real aunt. Uncle Jake just made you come here to take care of me."

"I'm not trying to replace your mother, sweetie."

"Don't call me sweetie." Sally tossed down the hand control to her game and turned her back.

Rachel ached for the little girl. She wished she knew how to take away her pain. What if by coming here, she'd caused Sally even more pain? Troubled, she made her way down the dark hall, praying for the Lord to heal the child's broken heart.

Intending to give Sally a little space before trying again, Rachel shouldered open the master bedroom door. Seeing the wide bed all made up and waiting steadied her. Sally's words hadn't rattled, her, had they?

No. The wedding dress shimmered like rich ivory, bringing back the memories of the day.

Rachel studied her new wedding band, glittering as pure and true as the vows she and Jake shared today. She remembered the affection in Jake's gaze, the comfort of his touch, the steady promise in his voice as he'd sworn to cherish her through this life.

I'm just feeling sad because he's not here, she realized, reaching for the dress. While she'd hoped for a much different night, she'd married a soldier and as a soldier's wife she realized there would be a lot of ways she would need to be extra supportive of him. Being okay about his call tonight was one of those ways.

She nudged the closet door open and searched for a hanger, which wasn't difficult considering the entire closet was empty. There wasn't a shirt or a hanger in sight on the bare rod.

Sally's words rolled back into her mind as she hustled across the hallway to the room where Jake's clothes hung. *Uncle Jake just made you come here to take care of me.*

That's not true. Rachel knew in her heart that it wasn't. So why then, had Jake planned for separate rooms for their wedding night?

Chapter Fifteen

Jake hauled his duffel out of the truck, slung the bag's thick strap over one shoulder and squinted against the rising sun. Exhausted, sweaty and limping, he hobbled up the steps to the back door. The first thing that greeted him was the scent of freshly brewing coffee and the greasy, meaty smell of cooked bacon. The second was fresh-faced, lovely Rachel in the kitchen.

His wife. That was hard to believe. The impossible knots tangled inside him yanked even more tightly—a warning sign. Danger ahead. He'd better get his emotions under control.

She was turned away from him, flipping pancakes. Her thick chestnut hair was swept back in a bouncy ponytail that swooped past her shoulder blades. She wore a pink tank top that showed off the graceful lines of her arms and her back, and wash-worn cutoffs hugged her slender hips. Her feet—toenails painted a pearled pink—were in a pair of pink flip-flops.

He'd never seen her like this. Relaxed, moving easily as she plated the pancakes and slipped them into the oven to keep warm. His heart turned over like an adoring dog and lay there, belly up and exposed.

Definitely danger ahead. He would not be weak. He would not be vulnerable. Panic set in because he didn't want to feel this way. Not in combat, not in life and never in love. Combat he was trained for but this— Lord, he didn't know how to leave the most vulnerable part of him exposed.

"You're back." He could tell that he'd startled her again, for her hand was over her heart and she sagged against the counter. "You're very good at being a stealthy Special Forces guy. I'm going to have to get used to that. You look exhausted. How about some coffee?"

Her hand was shaking as she poured a cup. Shaking. That's when he noticed she wasn't smiling. He didn't think he'd ever seen Rachel like this. Dimmed, as if she were holding back that light that always shone within her. She slipped the cup on the breakfast counter, pulling away before their fingers could meet. Turning away before he could do more than notice how sad she looked. *Sad*.

Then it was gone so fast, he wondered if he'd seen it at all. She looked tired, he realized. The stress of moving and leaving the responsibilities of her old life behind. And picking up those of a new one. He wanted to make this as easy on her as he could. "Coffee would be good. Figure you and I can take Sally to school, I'll show you around Fort Walton Beach. Show you where the grocery store is. The post office. That kind of thing. Maybe we can get in the walk I promised you last night."

"That sounds fine. Do you want breakfast?" She returned to the stove, where she poured more batter on the griddle.

She didn't seem fine; she didn't seem angry either. What did that mean? He didn't know. He was too tired to think. Every muscle he owned was killing him, he'd gotten out of shape since he'd been gone. It didn't take much. The ten-click run in full gear last night had taken a toll. "Is Sally up yet?"

"She's still sleeping. I think. She's refusing to talk to me."

"*What?* I thought she was looking forward to you being here."

"This is going to take some adjustment, Jake. I'm not her mother, and yet I'm telling her what to do and taking care of her. It's going to be hard."

"She wasn't rude to you, was she? She was so glad on the nanny's last day. I'll talk to her."

Rachel realized Jake didn't understand. Because he'd never been in Sally's position? Or because he saw his new wife as just another nanny with housekeeper skills? He couldn't be that cruel, right?

She flipped the pancakes, considering this man she'd thought was so wonderful. He *was* wonderful. Strong and decent and tender. His kisses were tender. A bad man didn't kiss like that, at least, she didn't think one could. His kisses felt like a perfect sunrise on a cold morning, chasing away the night shadows and giving light where there was none. They made her spirit lift like those quiet sweep of clouds at dawn, washed in a heavenly gold.

"Do I have a few minutes before breakfast is ready?"

She nodded as she checked the pancakes with the edge of the spatula. It was easier to concentrate on her cooking. Strange, this felt more like working in the diner than cooking for her family.

He set down his cup. Maybe he was going to kiss her now and hold her tight. Tell her how much he'd missed her. "Then I'm gonna grab a fast shower. Do I have ten minutes?"

She forced a nod, unable to believe her eyes as her new husband pivoted on his boot heel and bounded up the stairs, all soldier. But not a newlywed.

She already knew where he was going. As she sipped her coffee, she listened as his heavy step on the stairs without hesitation turned right and sounded directly overhead. He was not in the master bedroom, but the one where his clothes were. His room.

His room. She didn't understand. The diamonds on her left hand sparkled as if in celebration, tearing at her even more. He didn't use the shower in the main bathroom upstairs. She could hear the boards overhead squeaking slightly beneath his weight as he came and went. She heard the door to his room close, and she didn't understand. Married people shared a room. They were together. They were loving. If he didn't want to be with her, then what did that mean?

It means you may have made a mistake, Rachel. The sick feeling she'd been fighting all night returned. She flipped the last batch of pancakes, plated them and turned off the burner. She was hardly aware of anything but the footsteps overhead as Jake dressed and then ambled down the hallway. Coming closer.

She set out the last of the butter, moving woodenly, feeling cold inside because she knew what was coming. Whether they talked about it now or later tonight, it didn't matter. Nothing mattered but the truth.

The ring glittered, mockingly this time, taunting her as shame gathered in her stomach. She was married. That was a final, done deal. She'd vowed to honor this man before God, and so she would. The question was, what kind of marriage would this be? She'd been so eager to fulfill her dream that she'd accepted Jake's proposal without asking questions that now seemed vital.

He emerged from the shadows in the stairwell, looking heart-stoppingly handsome, striding easily toward her like a well-honed athlete. His cropped hair was jet-black, still wet from his shower, and his jaw was smooth-shaven. Even in jogging shorts and a tank, he looked fierce and capable, as though there wasn't anything he couldn't handle.

He did not look like the man who'd rescued her from Bullwinkle. Or who'd cradled a little grieving girl against his wide chest. Or a man who'd romanced her with roses and kindness and charm. That man was gone, she realized. A warrior was in his place, and she did not know this man. Was her Jake in there somewhere, she wondered, deep inside the toughness and steel?

"You are awesome, Rachel." He grabbed the syrup bottle she'd placed on the breakfast bar and upended it over his plate. One hard squeeze of his mighty hand was enough to make the maple sweetness shoot out like water. "I can't tell you how great this is. I'm starving. I am so glad I married you."

She felt the cup slip out of her clumsy fingers, but she didn't hear it hit the floor. Blood rushed through her ears, and like an ocean's tidal wave surging up to wash her away, it drowned out every sound. Jake looked startled, but she waved him away, emotion wedged in her throat so she couldn't speak. She grabbed at the roll of paper towels but tugged too hard and the roll jumped across the counter, unrolling as it went.

Her vision blurred as hot tears filled her eyes. A

voice inside her was saying, "He didn't mean that the way it sounded. This isn't as bad as you think." But it was.

She hadn't been married twenty-four hours and it was so different from what she'd thought. It fell so far short of what she'd imagined. There was no companionable happiness, no affection and conversation and togetherness, and the dream of it shattered at her feet and lay in pieces, right along with the cup.

"Baby, let me get that—"

"I've got it," she croaked, her voice sounding raw and broken as her dreams. Blinding hot tears scalded her eyes as she gave the paper towels another yank and this time the paper tore away. She had way too many lengths, but she didn't care. She wadded them up quite as if she saw them, as if everything were perfectly fine, and knelt at Jake's feet to swipe up the mess. Ceramic edges clanked together as she swiped. "Go on and finish your meal."

"No, you aren't fine." He knelt and she could feel the tender wave of his concern. He was so close, she could lean forward a few inches and she'd be able to lay her cheek on the chest she knew felt as solid as steel. But she would not lay her troubles there. She could not find the words to tell him her fears. Or how foolish she'd been.

"This is about me leaving last night. It was unfortunate timing."

"Trust me, that is not an issue. I told you I understood. I knew about your commitment to this country when I agreed to marry you." But what about his commitment to her? This was a man who'd swept her off her feet, told her how wonderful she was, told her everything she'd wanted to hear. It was a man who'd stood before God and vowed to honor and cherish her, to love her and care for her. Surely he'd meant that. Surely he had.

She blinked back every tear. Swiped up every piece of ceramic and coffee spill, feeling as if she were mopping up what was left of her lost dreams, too.

"Tell me. Please." Jake took the sodden paper towels and broken shards from her and set them on the counter. He towered over her, so strong and distant and remote. Then held out his hand to help her up.

Oh, it felt right when her palm met his. The twist of her heart. The sigh of her soul. It was a new day, this would be their first full day as man and wife. Surely, she could trust him. She came into his arms, he folded her close, and she was home. "I guess I need reassuring."

"Then I'm you're man. What do you need, baby?"

Oh, she liked it when he talked like that, with his voice a low rumble in his throat. "I noticed how your things were in the extra bedroom and then Sally had said you'd married me just to take care of her."

She felt him stiffen. She heard his heartbeat flutter. He wasn't saying anything.

This can't be right. She pushed away from him and kept going. A cold chill swept through her, and she shivered as hard as if she'd stepped out into a Montana blizzard without a coat on. "You didn't marry me to be a nanny, right? This is a real marriage. You'll be with me, tonight, forever, right?"

"Rachel, I thought we would both need our space. That's all. I can move my stuff back."

"That's not what I want. Not like this. You're acting as if this is a convenient arrangement, something practical and sensible because you're leaving in two weeks and you'll be gone for the next six months. Tell me that's not true." She watched his eyes harden. Felt the answer in his silence.

The tiniest hope within her faded. Despair shrouded her like a cocoon. Everything around her seemed distant and dim and muffled. Everything within her turned to ice until there was no pain, only a void where no wishes live, and no dreams prosper.

"It's not exactly true." His words sounded choked, as if he were in great pain, too. "I can't lie to you, Rachel. I value you too much."

"Value me? You married me to watch your niece and cook your meals. You sent me roses. You romanced me. You made me fall in love with you and believe that I was special to you. That I was your one true love."

He broke at the sight of her tears. What had happened? He would never want to hurt her. He hadn't hurt her, not really, and yet tears pooled in her eyes and he could feel her heartbreak as mightily as if he'd taken a bullet in the chest for her. He would take a bullet for her, he would protect her with his life. But he could not make her understand. "There is no such thing as true love. I've been all around the globe, and I haven't seen it."

She recoiled as if he'd slapped her in the face, and he couldn't say why but he could feel the shock of it in her battered heart—her heart that he was hurting.

That wasn't what he wanted. He wanted to keep her safe and protect her. To shelter her and make her happy. He'd married her, he would give her all he could.

Except your heart, a tiny voice inside him whispered. And it was the truth. A truth he could not deny. He'd shielded up his heart so well, that not war or evil or the horrors he'd witnessed could touch it. Only this woman and her gentle kindness had come close. He'd protected his heart so long, he didn't know if he could do anything else.

All he knew for sure was that he could feel Rachel's hurt as surely as the ocean breeze on his face and hear her heartbreak in the brittle sound of the palm leaves overhead. The bright blue Gulf shimmered like jewels in the first sunlight and he swiped the pain from his eyes. He had to fix this. He took a step toward her, sure that all he needed to do was to comfort her in his arms.

She took two steps back, looking up at him as if he was a stranger she didn't know.

He definitely had to fix that. "You are special to me. More than I know how to say. Don't you know that I'd do anything for you, anything you need?"

"Then tell me that you love me. Really love me. Tell me the truth."

He could not say the words. He was afraid that they would diminish him, tear down the core of steel he had to have to be a good soldier. But he wanted to. He wished he could surrender. "I've loved you more than I've ever loved anyone."

"That's not the same."

"I'll do my best to be a good husband to you, but you know that it's not roses and horse rides and starlight, right? Any marriage is a practical arrangement."

"A practical arrangement?" She said the words with a look of horror twisting across her beautiful face. A face that did not stop gazing up at him with all the light draining from her loving eyes, and taking that affection with it.

Failure shattered him. He was failing at this, the most significant thing that had ever happened to him. This woman was his wife, the woman who meant more than anything, and he was failing her. Failure was not an option in his world. Nor was softness. *Help me, Lord. I'm drowning here.*

Her eyes were liquid sadness. She turned away from

him and his silence and all the words he could not say and things he could not be and stared down the beach. Two units down, the neighbor was noisily putting up a six-foot ladder. The aluminum clang echoed like a gunshot over the hush of the tide on the shore. The guy was putting Christmas lights on a palm tree in his yard. His wife came outside, holding two cups of coffee, and told him in a soft voice to be quiet. His answer was goodhearted, but the breeze carried his words away.

Jake felt his world fracture even more as he watched his neighbor hop down from the ladder to join his pretty wife at their small patio table. *That's* what he wanted, that kind of closeness, that connection, and he was afraid of it. He could admit that now. Afraid to place so much stock in something that could not be seen or conquered, only felt. Afraid to take down the shield that had kept him safe through over a decade in his career and leave his heart and soul completely unprotected.

He took a few steps after her out of the open doorway and onto the cement patio. How did he do it? How did he start? The titanium he'd closed around his heart began to buckle. "I didn't want to rush you."

"What?" She turned to study him over her shoulder, confusion on her face and tears on her cheeks.

I made her cry. Nothing could seem more horrible. He didn't want to hurt Rachel ever. He would never do so again. He took a step toward her, the warrior in him unable to figure out how to attack and win this fight.

He'd need his heart for that. His whole heart, un-shielded and vulnerable. "The separate bedrooms. I rushed you into marriage. I wasn't sure if you would be ready for a real wedding night."

"That you even have to ask that is so wrong." She only seemed more upset. "Do you understand? I thought you married me to love me. I thought you saw in me—" Her face twisted in sheer agony and she turned her back on him. Her hands went to her face and her shoulders shook. That you saw in me someone to truly love.

How could she tell him that? He didn't understand, she'd seen that clearly on his face. He thought she'd be grateful for a practical arrangement. It made sense, she realized. It all made sense. How he overlooked her faults and asked the right questions to find out how des-perately she just wanted to be married.

What she did not tell him was how sacred she be-lieved marriage to be. She meant her vows, heart and soul, those vows that were the strongest on earth. To love and cherish through hardship and trial, to find love in your heart without fail.

And he wanted a nanny and a cook. The sunrise splashed stunning bright colors across the waiting sky, and the pure golden light that followed dawn seemed to mock her, for she felt as if there could be no more sunshine in her world, no more beautiful days and bright clear skies. How could she have made such a monumental mistake?

"Rachel?" He was behind her, his hand on her shoulder, his touch more calming than anything on this earth. He leaned close and she shivered with longing for what could not be.

His lips brushed her cheek as he spoke quietly, as if they were in church, as if they were the only two people on a beach in paradise. "I love you."

"But you said—" She choked on a sob. She couldn't believe him, not anymore. He'd tricked her, or so it seemed. But maybe she'd tricked herself in believing in fairy tales to begin with.

"I want my happily-ever-after to be with you, Rachel Hathaway." His voice sounded strangled, and his strong hands caught her around the waist and turned her in his arms. "I married you for Sally, it's true, but I married you for me even more. I n-need you."

"N-no," she sputtered on a heart-wrenching sob. "You want a p-practical m-marriage."

"Only because I'm dumb and I thought it would be safer. But I'm starting to get this marriage thing." Jake shook all over. He'd never done anything so terrifying in his life. But for Rachel's happiness, he would do anything, even tell her the truth that terrified him.

He would show her the part of him that he trusted to no one. The shields fell, all defenses were abandoned. He could not protect his heart at the cost of hers. "I love you more than my pride or my life or my very being, and it scares me. More than anything ever has. Can you understand that?"

The sadness ebbed from her beautiful eyes.

"Nothing in my life—no one—could ever mean as much to me as you. I love you. I'll say that as many times as it takes for you to believe it. I intend to honor and cherish you, above myself, above all my fears and my stubborn pride. I am trusting you with my heart. Can we make this marriage of ours all you've dreamed of?"

"I think it already is. Now." The warm ocean lapped at her toes as the hush of the morning seemed to reassure her. She saw her future being loved by this strong, tender man. His kiss was like paradise; his embrace like eternity. She thanked the Lord for this beautiful dream of love come true.

Jake took her hand and led her through the sand toward the open sliding door, where Sally would need to be woken up and breakfast eaten. The demands of the day remained but for them, there were only blue skies ahead.

* * * * *

Dear Reader,

THE McKASLIN CLAN continues when Rachel meets her brother's best friend. Jake is on temporary leave from active duty in the Middle East so that he can take guardianship of his orphaned niece. Rachel falls in love with both the man and the little girl, and forsakes the life she knows in Montana to move across the country to where Jake is stationed. Always a romantic, Rachel marries her knight in shining armor and means her wedding vows with every bit of her heart and soul. Love, like faith, takes great belief and trust. But will her love be strong enough to open Jake's battle weary heart?

Thank you for choosing *Blessed Vows*. I hope you enjoy Rachel's story as much as I've enjoyed writing it.

I wish you joy and the sweetest of blessings,

Jillian Hart

Don't miss Jillian Hart's next
Inspirational romance, A HANDFUL OF HEAVEN,
available February 2006.
If you liked FAITH ON THE LINE
from Love Inspired, you'll love the
FAITH AT THE CROSSROADS *continuity series,*
beginning in January in Love Inspired Suspense!
And now, turn the page for a sneak preview of
A TIME TO PROTECT by Lois Richer,
the first installment of
FAITH AT THE CROSSROADS.
On sale in January 2006 from Steeple Hill Books.

Brendan Montgomery switched his beeper to Vibrate and slid it back inside his shirt pocket. Nothing was going to spoil Manuel DeSantis Vance's first birthday party—and this large Vance and Montgomery gathering—if he could help it.

Peter Vance's puffed out chest needed little explanation. He was as formidable as any father proudly displaying his beloved child. Peter's wife Emily waited on Manuel's other side, posing for the numerous photographs Yvette Duncan insisted posterity demanded. Apparently posterity was greedy.

Judging by the angle of her camera, Brendan had a hunch Yvette's lens sidetracked from the parents to the cake she'd made for Manuel. Who could blame her? That intricate train affair must have taken hours to create and assemble, and little Manuel obviously appreciated her efforts.

"Make sure you don't chop off their heads this time, Yvette." As the former mayor of Colorado Springs, Frank Montgomery had opinions on everything. And as Yvette's mentor, he'd never been shy about offering her his opinion, especially on all aspects of picture-taking. But since Yvette's camera happened to be the latest in digital technology and Frank had never owned one, Brendan figured most of his uncle's free advice was superfluous and probably useless. But he wouldn't be the one to tell him so.

"Don't tell me what to do, Frank," Yvette ordered, adjusting the camera. "Just put your arm around your wife. Liza, can you get him to smile?" Satisfied, Yvette motioned for Dr. Robert Fletcher and his wife Pamela, who were Manuel's godparents, and their two young sons, to line up behind the birthday boy.

Brendan eased his way into the living room and found a horde of Montgomery and Vance family members lounging around the room, listening to a news report on the big-screen television.

"Alistair Barclay, the British hotel mogul now infamous for his ties to a Latin-American drug cartel, died today under suspicious circumstances. Currently in jail, Barclay was accused of running a branch of the notorious crime syndicate right here in Colorado Springs. The drug cartel originated in Venezuela under the direction of kingpin Baltasar Escalante, whose private plane crashed some months ago while he was attempting to escape the CIA. Residents of Colorado Springs have worked long and hard to free their city from the grip of crime—"

"Hey, guys, this is a party. Let's lighten up." Brendan reached out and pressed the mute button, followed by a chorus of groans. "You can listen to the same newscast tonight, but we don't want to spoil Manuel's big day with talk of drug cartels and death, do we?"

His brother Quinn winked and took up his cause. "Yeah, what's happened with that cake, anyway? Are we ever going to eat it? I'm starving."

"So is somebody else, apparently," Yvette said, appearing in the doorway, her flushed face wreathed in a grin. "Manuel already got his thumb onto the train track and now he's covered in black icing. His momma told him he had to wait 'till the mayor gets here, though, so I guess you'll just have to do the same, Quinn."

Good-natured groans filled the room.

"Maxwell Vance has been late since he got elected into office," Fiona Montgomery said, her eyes dancing with fun. "Maybe one of us should give him a call and remind him his grandson is waiting for his birthday cake. In fact, I'll do it myself."

"Leave the mayor alone, Mother. He already knows your opinion on pretty much everything," Brendan said, sharing a grin with Quinn.

"It may be that the mayor has been delayed by some important meeting." Alessandro Donato spoke up from his seat in the corner. "After Thanksgiving, that is the time when city councilors and mayors iron out their budgets, yes?"

"But just yesterday I talked to our mayor about that, in regard to a story I'm doing on city finances." Brendan's cousin Colleen sat cross-legged on the floor, her hair tied back in the ponytail she eternally favored. "He said they hadn't started yet."

Something about the way Alessandro moved when he heard Colleen's comment sent a nerve in Brendan's neck to twitching, enough to make him take a second look at the man. Moving up through the ranks of the FBI after his time as a police officer had only happened because Brendan usually paid attention to that nerve. Right now it was telling him to keep an eye on the tall, lean man named Alessandro, even if he *was* Lidia Vance's nephew.

There was something about Alessandro that didn't quite fit. What was the story on this guy anyway?

A phone rang. Brendan chuckled when everyone in the room checked their pockets. The grin faded when Alessandro spoke into his. His face paled, his body tensed. He murmured one word, then listened.

"Hey, something's happening! Turn up the TV, Brendan," Colleen said. Everyone was staring at the screen where a reporter stood in front of city hall.

Brendan raised the volume.

"Mayor Vance was apparently on his way to a family event when the shot was fired. Excuse me, I'm getting an update." The reporter lifted one hand to press the earpiece closer. "I'm told there may have been more than one shot fired. As I said, at this moment, Maxwell Vance is on his way to the hospital. Witnesses say he was bleeding profusely from his head and chest, though we have no confirmed details. We'll update you as the situation develops."